The Vi-Purrs

by Jeanne Foguth

Acknowledgements, Etc.

As most of my followers know, Xander de Hunter is a tribute to Rom, who was the greatest cat ever. I am sure many of you will disagree because you know a certain feline, who is so far superior that s/he is surely 'the greatest cat ever', so perhaps it would be more accurate for me to say that Rom was the greatest cat I ever knew. Rom passed away at the age of 16.5, and had an amazing talent for using technology (we used to think he was a feline 007). Since this is a tribute to Rom, Xander de Hunter's skills with technology are exceptional, as is all of Catamondo, a world I never imagined existed, prior to beginning The Red Claw.

While Rom was my 'greatest cat ever', many others feel the same way about their beloved pets, which are gone. Pauline Nicolaï recently lost her dear Footie due to health issues. Sixteen years never seems like enough when you have a wonderful furry-friend. Footie was a smart little black and white cat. I am dedicating The Vi-Purrs to Footie and brought back Sharkey, another smart black and white cat in Footie's honor.

Many thanks to my faithful beta readers, Kaj, Kensleigh, Paul, Marcha Fox and Pauline Nicolaï without whom my work would have 'rogue commas' and 'renegade spelling', not to mention strange formatting anomalies. Thank you also to Kiara Graham for her prowess with digital design and The Vi-Purrs' cover.

Cataloging in Publication Data is on file with the Library of Congress.

ISBN 978-0-9913339-0-5 Copyright 2016

Books by Jeanne Foguth

Kazza's Sci-fi Chatterre Trilogy:

Star Bridge

Thunder Moon

Fire Island

Fantasy

Xander's Sea Purrtector Files:

Latitudes and Cattitudes (prequel to the Sea Purrtector Files)

The Red Claw

Purr-a-noia

The Vi-Purrs

Me-YEOW!

Contemporary Suspense/Romance

Deadly Rumors

Fatal Attractions

Passion's Fire

Chapter 1

"That's perfect!" Ginny told Mischief, who was balancing on the bogie board. "Hold it right there." Ginny began snapping pictures, which would undoubtedly appear on Whispurring Winds' blog. In the two months since they had adopted the little calico, everyone's life had been turned upside down.

And Ginny's blog had gained an unexpected model for the boating life of a water-loving kitten.

Xander peered over Ginny's shoulder and studied Mischief's posture. She had easily adapted to living aboard Whispurring Winds and had the potential to become an excellent Sea Purrtector, but she needed to learn to keep a lower profile. His tail smacked the cockpit's royal blue cushion in frustration. When he had recommended adopting her, he'd assumed he would obtain an apprentice, not a tadpole. His ears flattened. Most days, she hurried through her lessons, so she could get outside and get wet; he suspected her water obsession was real and not an act for Ginny's camera. Why else did she leap overboard to swim ashore, instead of ride in the dingy? Moreover, why did she scurry out onto the deck when it rained? The very thought of being out in a tropical thunderstorm without a valid reason made his pristine seal-point fur threaten to stand on end. A low growl startled him, but when Ginny glanced at him, he realized the sound had come from him.

Xander gulped. How had the kitten undermined his self-control?

Ginny looked past him, her gaze searching the anchorage for the source of the growl, then, with a shrug, her attention returned to Mischief posing on the gently rocking bogie board. Xander hopped down and headed to the salon, his thoughts centered on how he could continue the kick-boxing portion of Mischief's training without convincing Mike and Ginny that they needed to purrtect her from what they seemed to think was a jealousy attack.

Watching Mischief waste time, which she should be using to study, was also wasting his time and undermining his control. Xander went below to catch up on his correspondence, but after several minutes of being unable to concentrate on his email, he Skyped Merlin. Seconds later, his best buddy's emerald eyes were studying him. "Hey Pal, what's wrong?"

"The water nymph is wasting everyone's time with a bogie board lesson."

Merlin's ears perked with interest. "Sounds fun."

Of course the white Norwegian Forest Cat would think so; he loved getting wet, too. "Want to come down here and get her to learn kickboxing, spelling, math and history?"

Merlin's whiskers stiffened. "Nope. No thanks, though I wouldn't mind helping her with swimming lessons."

Xander growled.

Merlin asked, "Did you ever get that Vi-Purr situation resolved? The Daily Mews keeps reporting about chupacabra sightings and attacks, and we know those misfits are actually doing the dirty deeds."

"Between trying to get Mischief to study and do her homework, I haven't had time to keep up with anything other than you, Fluffy and the Catamondo alerts."

"All you've written about in the last month is Mischief and how having an apprentice isn't what you expected. Dude, she's a kitten, and she's acting like a kitten. Eventually, she'll grow up, but in the meantime, you might as well enjoy the consequences of your choices."

Enjoy? His best friend's emerald green eyes sparkled with amusement and much as he hated to admit it, Merlin was probably correct about Mischief. For certain, having her here was his choice and he certainly could not let others know that he was having doubts about that decision. Had Merlin recognized that Mischief shared his fondness for water sports and being in front of a camera? Not that Merlin ever admitted that he liked being photographed, but no cat could spend years being the poster boy for the top brand of cat food and not like their job.

When he didn't say anything, Merlin said, "Did you ever find all those loony Haitian cats? I'm talking about the ones the forensic team couldn't account for."

"Haven't had time."

"All work and no play..." Merlin leaned close to the camera and whispurred, "Been to any more voodoo ceremonies? How about that Damon-demon-dude? Did you ever figure out if he was actually a zombie priest or something demonic?" Merlin's expression became serious. "He's one I'd like to know, for certain, what happened, too."

"I'm sure he was one of the ones that died in the fire, when the lab burned."

Merlin raised a brow. "But his remains were never positively identified, were they?"

Xander shook his head.

"Also, did you ever figure out how Lucy Fur was involved?"

Again, Xander shook his head.

"Did you hear that the Counsel is being cautious about the information they share with her?" Merlin settled back to his original position. "And how come they had so much catnip? What was going on with that?"

Despite his growing worry that the Moreau situation might not be totally resolved, Xander smiled at his best friend's phrasing. Merlin liked to pretend he was a brainless beach bum, but was actually very well-read and smart as a whip. Merlin was also infatuated with Purrsident Mitzi Montgomery's purrsonal assistant, Cheyenne, so his sudden interest in finding out details about the Haitian mission could be because Merlin wanted an excuse to contact her. Of course, there was also the possibility that Cheyenne was using Merlin to give him a message because she knew someone higher up in Catamondo's ruling cats wanted to know why a case that should be closed still showed enough odd activity to make an occasional headline.

Xander swished his tail as he realized that despite Merlin's obsession with Cheyenne, he also had valid questions that needed solid answers. And figuring out those answers would be good training for little Ms. Photogenic, which was probably what Merlin had already figured out. "You're right, I need to focus on answers to your questions."

Merlin nodded.

In the distance, he heard the familiar drone of the dinghy's outboard motor approaching, which meant that Mike was back from fishing. What would they have for lunch? Lobster or fish? Tail swishing in anticipation, Xander quickly told Merlin he'd keep in touch, then logged off and left the computer exactly as he'd found it. Then, he went back into the cockpit, sprawled on the sun-warmed cushion he'd recently left, closed his eyes and pretended to be asleep. Shortly after the dinghy docked, his nose declared that the fish-du-jour was on the grill.

When Ginny went below to make the rest of the meal, Mischief pranced up to him. "I know you're not asleep."

Opening an eye, he saw that her white, charcoal and gold fur was soaking wet. "Fall in?" She shrugged. "On purpose?"

She giggled. "Would I do that?"

"You know that fish use the ocean for a bathroom, right?" Her pretty little pink nose wrinkled. He sat up and stretched. "Think about all that fish pee, next time you groom your coat."

"You're mean."

"I'm telling you facts you should already know." Mischief shook her body, but only three small drops fell to the deck. "You'd be wise to roll on a towel to get as much water off as possible." He tipped an ear to the beach towel Ginny had left on the captain's seat.

"But that's not my towel."

"Then dry off whatever way you want."

She hopped onto the captain's seat and began to roll on Ginny's favorite pink-hibiscus towel.

"Have you talked to your mother or Garfield recently?" Xander prodded.

"You know we skyped, yesterday. Why?"

"Just wondered if they said anything about your Aunt Lucy."

Mischief stopped rolling and stared at him. "Yes, as a matter of fact, they said that they haven't heard a word about her in the past six weeks, and that is really, really strange because she loves being in the headlines... but you know that, don't you?"

"About the headlines?" She nodded. Xander inclined his head and said, "You have mentioned it, previously."

Mischief sat up and stared across the cockpit at him. "Have you been spying on me?"

"Why would I do that?" he asked, startled.

"I don't know, but it is what you do."

"I watch, I do not spy."

She snorted. "Poe-tay-toe – Po-tah-toe."

Though he was tempted to box her ears, he knew he was older, smarter and more skilled, so he refused to allow her to distract him. "My interest is in your aunt, who – as you just pointed out – is not behaving in her typical pattern and since she is the Dominican Republic Purrtector, I need to find out why."

"Seriously?" Mischief wiggled with excitement. "How do we do that?"

"If you know anyone in her Purrtectorate, who we can contact, that would be good, but mainly I think we need to motivate our crew to relocate."

"You realize August is the hottest month, right?"

"Why?" While it was warm, Whispurring Winds was pleasant, as it rode its anchor, nose pointed into the breeze.

"Well, if I understand the science that you've been trying to teach me, here, on the boat, it's cooler because the water is cooler than the ground."

Xander nodded.

"Well, won't it be hotter on land? And didn't you say that cities are hotter and nastier than here?"

"All true, but we can't solve every problem from here."

"I heard Santo Domingo was as stinky and icky as Port-au-Prince." She gave a dramatic shiver. "I don't wanna go there."

"Why do you assume that is our destination?"

"Well because I thought you wanted to investigate Tante Lucy." He nodded. "And The Daily Mews always writes about what she's doing in Santo Domingo." She gave him a look that suggested that he might be getting a tad senile.

He smiled. "Exactly, The Mews hasn't been writing about her – in fact, it has not had a single article about her since we sighted her at Étang Saumâtre." Xander raised a brow. "Think about that. Then, think about the fact that her file states that her actual home is Jimaní, which is in Independencia Province, not far from where we observed that meeting. I suspect she is still there."

"But why?"

"Don't know, but do know that Jimaní is a main thoroughfare between Haiti and The Dominican Republic."

"But why would she be there when she loves being in the news so much?"

"That is an excellent question and one I want answered." Xander stood up. "Now, are you ready for lunch? Smells like the fish is done."

She hopped off the seat and scampered into the lounge, hopped onto the built-in settee, then quickly curled up in the corner, where she promptly gave every impression of being asleep. Ginny glanced at the lounge from the galley, where she was making two salads and some pasta, noticed Mischief with her tiny paw over one eye, smiled, then turned back to cutting an avocado.

Good Hathor, did his sous chef actually believe any cat could fall asleep with damp fur?

How intelligent were humans?

Xander hopped to the left, landing on the seat under the radio and settled down a moment before Mike ceremoniously placed a platter of perfectly grilled fillets on the table. Almost simultaneously, Ginny leaned over the settee back and put two place settings on the table, then turned back for the two bowls of salad and a basket of bread.

Both of Xander's brows raised, as he noted that she had not served him, first. Then, as if reading his mind, she handed Mike his special dish. Mike put the biggest filet on it, then placed it in front of him. That was more like it!

As Mike and Ginny sat down to eat, Mischief pretended to wake. Of course, they then had to fuss over her and hand feed her tiny bits of fish by hand. Xander didn't know who was more to blame, Mischief for playing them or his humans for being suckers. What was even worse, he realized that this was all his fault because he was the one who had made the decision to take on an apprentice. "Enjoy the attention while you can," he said, with his mouth full.

"Are you jealous?" she asked.

"Of course not. But you'll probably wish you actually had been taking a nap when you think about the fact that you spent all afternoon posing on that silly bogie board, then you are taking ten times as long to eat because they think they need to feed you like a helpless baby."

"You are jealous!"

He swallowed. "No, just thinking about all the research you skipped and the training you avoided, which still needs to get done if you expect to advance to the next level."

"You know I'm capable and smart. What does it matter?"

"If you assume that I will forge test scores to send to Training Council, think again. My reputation means a lot to me."

"But I read the assignment."

"Which one? And when?"

"A couple days ago."

"Have you logged into your home-study course since then?"

"It's not like that is real school."

"Isn't it?"

She shook her head. "Real school is when we go to a special place and there's a real teacher, like Professor Meowingtons."

"Ah, the esteemed professor." He should have figured out why she was shirking her lessons. "Would it surprise you to learn that the home-study course you're enrolled in is the same one most diplomates' kittens attend and that real teachers, like your beloved Professor Meowingtons, grade the homework? That they are the ones who decide if you pass or not?"

Her leaf-green eyes got big as saucers. "Seriously?"

"Have I ever lied to you?"

"No." Matted fur and dinner forgotten, she jumped down and scurried to the aft cabin, where her notepad was. Ginny and Mike looked from her to him, brows furrowed. Pleased with his small success, Xander returned to eating the purrfectly prepared fillet and began planning the best way to find answers for Merlin's questions.

"Well," said Mike, "I guess she was full."

"Maybe she had too much sun and doesn't feel well," Ginny said. "Did you notice that she didn't even groom herself properly?"

"She did look silly with her fur in tufts," Mike said.

Ginny nodded. "Do you think she's sick?"

"If she isn't herself by tomorrow, perhaps we should find a vet...." Mike frowned. "It's probably not healthy for her to drink sea water, and you know she must be getting that in her system when she cleans her fur."

"True, but it won't be easy keeping her away from the water... Have you ever seen a kitten who loved water and swimming quite so much?"

Mike shook his head.

Xander had never understood Merlin's fascination with the wet stuff, either, but over the years had learned to accept it and even learned basic swimming and surfing skills from his pal. After he had been named the first Sea Purrtector, he had wondered if meeting Merlin was kismet. In truth, Merlin would have been the ideal Sea Purrtector, but he had made sure that everyone just thought he was a gorgeous white Norwegian, who was the ideal representative for gourmet food. Only a select few knew about the skills, which made him an excellent Purrtector. Now, Xander wondered if Mischief and her water obsession was another example of fate, since water skills were something Sea Purrtectors should have.

But with the sorry state of her grades, would she ever graduate from her bright red flea collar to wear the high-tech, sapphire collar of Sea Purrtector?

He swished his tail at the honor of training his successor. Perhaps she was correct in pursuing bogie board skills, but that didn't mean he could allow her to shirk her normal lessons.

After dinner, Xander sat down with his computer to learn as much as possible about Lucy Fur, then he began researching Jimaní in the Dominican Republic's Independencia Province, where she had last been seen. What he found were several references to supposed chupacabra attacks in that area. Could those relate to Lucy Fur and the Moreau problems he'd discovered on the shores of Étang Saumâtre? Xander frowned and wondered if Jimaní being a main thoroughfare between Haiti and The Dominican Republic could be significant. And if so, why?

Also, why had Doctor Moreau been creating freaks and clones of important cats in her lab? And why had she been drying tons of catnip? Even though that case was supposedly closed, Merlin was correct about there being too many unanswered questions. The worst being, confirming what had happened to the Damon. Plan made, he quickly composed an email to Merlin:

Hi Mer-man,

Did you ever find a birth record for a tom answering the Damon's description? I haven't had any luck.

I am planning a trip back to Étang Saumâtre, where I hope to discover if there is a connection between it and Jimaní, D.R. Obviously, I'm looking for the link between Lucy Fur, the D.R. Purrtector and Damon and/or the Moreau operation. I think you're correct about there being potential loose ends and too many questions left unanswered. One being how the Vi-Purrs escaped. I mean they must have, because it's the only way to explain why there have been so many 'chupacabra' sightings.

To answer the questions you posed, before Mike's return cut our chat short:

No, I was never able to figure out exactly what Damon is or was because his body was never identified, but I am almost positive that he was a product of the Moreau operation. And, before you ask, no, I never confirmed what their ultimate goal was, but the only thing that makes sense is that they were after power and control. I suspect they

were using the catnip to cloud the senses of as many cats as possible –
it is a lot easier to get away with stuff if the catarazzi are watching
fools howling at the moon, instead of asking why there is so much
herb around. Sadly, cats like Jacques, love the stuff and will even
work for it.

Xander studied what he'd written and wrinkled his nose at the idea of
any cat allowing their honor to be compromised over an herb. While
he liked the way catnip repelled mosquitoes and other biting bugs, he
had never understood why so many made such a fuss over it. For that
matter, he had never understood those silly fake mice, either. Had
whatever human designed the things ever seen an actual mouse?
Surely not, since those things had nothing in common with any
mouse, living or dead. And yet, humans kept making the things and
kittens kept playing with them. Had Dr. Moreau planned to use the
herb in some diabolical plot?

If not, why had there been so much herb drying?

Had he totally thwarted her, as he had initially believed, or were there
loose ends?

Who would know?

Rufus came to mind and with that thought, came the glimmer of a
plan.

Chapter 2

"What do you mean – I need to act sick?" Mischief demanded.
Xander flattened his seal-point ears. How dare she question his judgement! "Just that – pretend you don't feel well."
"Because?"
Her threatening tone and belligerent attitude had his tail whipping. How dare she question his instructions! "The objective is to get a trip to the vet," he said through clenched jaws.
She let out a fur-fluffing reow. "Oh, no, no, no, no, no! I've been there once and they jabbed me with needles and I've heard that even worse things happen there." She took a step backward and nearly fell off the settee. "If you want someone to go to the vet, you pretend to be sick!" she growled.
"Fine, I will." He flattened his ears and leaned forward until their noses touched. "IF you use my stay there as cover to go to Étang Saumâtre BY YOURSELF and make sure the investigative team didn't miss anything in the burned lab." He glared at her. "And after you're done checking that out, you need to go to Jimaní to see what connection you can find – if any – between the Moreau operation and your dear aunt Lucy Fur, plus determine if the chupacabra sightings have anything to do with the Mor-"

"Why?" Mischief swallowed. Though her voice quivered, anger still sparked in her leaf-green eyes and her calico coat bristled, declaring she was ready to fight.

"Because there seem to be loose ends. For one thing, the forensic crew didn't find enough bodies." Xander resisted the urge to sharpen his claws on the upholstery. "There are too many questions left unanswered." His tail smacked the settee. "And, as you said, in the past six weeks your esteemed aunt has not filed a single report with the Council, nor has she been in a single headline or anywhere in The Daily Mews and that is very strange." He sat back and took a calming breath.

"Yes, it is." Her nose suddenly paled. "Do you think she was one of the dead bodies?"

"If, and I repeat IF that is true, a new DR Purrtector needs to be appointed until the next election." Why hadn't he considered the possibility that Lucy Fur could have slipped into the lab and be among the dead? While he doubted this was fact, it was another thing he needed to investigate. "Now, are you beginning to understand why I need to investigate further and you need to go to the vet as a diversion?"

"She is MY aunt, I should check on her."

For a moment, Xander's eyes involuntarily crossed and his vision blurred. Had there ever been such a stubborn kitten? "Mischief, it is my job to investigate this sort of thing," he said carefully enunciating each word. "You do not have the training or skills." Her eyes narrowed, and he knew she intended to argue, so he quickly added, "I expect that you will eventually be an excellent Purrtector, but right now, you are a three month old kitten, who I need to purrtect."

"I'm four and I can purrtect myself!"

Xander clamped his jaws shut. If Fluffy was correct, his apprentice wouldn't become a calm, civilized cat for another year and a half, and currently her age was equivalent to a six-year-old human, which meant that she thought she was immortal and the center of the universe. He suspected the next eighteen months would seem like a lifetime.

When he didn't argue, Mischief began to look uncertain. "How am I supposed to learn to be a Purrtector if I'm getting stuck with needles at the vet's?"

"That will come with time and training." He patiently answered, then his eyes narrowed as he added, "Your efforts with the latter, since coming here, have been less than sterling."

"I turned in my homework."

"I know."

"Then why'd you suggest that I didn't?"

"Because I know how smart you are and what your potential is and while the work I saw fulfilled the basic assignment, it was more of a slap-dash to get it out of the way so you could do something else."

"Is that so bad?"

"You dare ask?"

"Well, that Moreau stuff was supposed to be your investigation and you left and now you say you have to go back there to make sure things are right." She had the nerve to narrow her eyes and bristle her whiskers.

"If I hadn't needed to bring you back to your mother, I would have stayed there to oversee the forensic team."

"I don't think so."

"Excuse me?"

"You heard me and do NOT use me as an excuse for whatever it is that you don't think got done right."

He sank his claws into the royal blue seat-cushion so he couldn't smack her. Were all kittens psycho or just this water-loving spitfire?

"Will you please agree to pretend to be ill?"

"Well, now that you've finally asked me nicely instead of try to order me, yes."

Unbelievable! "Thank you."

With a smirk and swish of her tail, she went onto the deck and sprawled in a sun puddle.

~0~

As Mike drove the rental car over the potholes toward Port-au-Prince, Xander sat in the backseat and watched the scenery pass. One of Haiti's tap-tap buses zoomed by in the opposite direction, leaving behind the memory of a blur of vivid colors and a fog of exhaust. A quick glance assured him that Mike had the air on recirculate. Even so, Mischief sneezed. Xander looked at her. Mischief was lying in her hot pink travel crate and trying to look as pitiful as possible. "I didn't realize your nose was so sensitive."

She sneezed, again. "Garfield's human always joked about it." She sneezed, a third time. "He's my vet, you know."

"No, I didn't. Why didn't you mention that, previously?" He tapped his collar, so he could make mental notes and not overlook any other potentially important details.

"I would have, if you'd asked."

The urge to smack her was nearly overpowering, but his skills were equal to the task and he certainly was not about to do something that would have her go all ninja on him and blow her sickly act. So, in case Mike or Ginny looked back at them, he laid down, chin on paws and stared at her, as if he was worried sick about her. "Is there anything else you can think of, which might be relevant and helpful for me to know?"

"Well, just that Sharkey said she would try to meet us at my mom's."

It took all his willpower to remain calm. "Why would Sharkey meet us there?"

"Because I knew that address and gave it to her."

"Fine, but why would she come to Haiti? Isn't she still training in Jamaica?"

"If you paid as much attention to The Daily Mews as you do those boring security reports, you would realize she graduated and was given a posting in Puerto Rico." Mischief flicked her ear.

"If she is supposed to be in Puerto Rico, why do you think she'd stop by your mom's?"

Mischief's nostrils flared. "Because she doesn't need to report for three weeks and Haiti is on route."

"Really?" He scratched his ear and wondered why her information sounded 'off'.

Mischief nodded, as much as was possible, while trying to act listless. "Yes, really."

With a flick of his claw, he keyed his collar to give him information on Sharkey. As he frequently did, he noticed the superiority of

Catamondo's information retrieval system over the humans' google system. Purrhaps one day, humans would managed to make their own systems as compact, efficient and portable as Catamondo's. Then, he added additional requests for updates on any new information about his destination, Lucy Fur, Damon, chupacabras, the Dominican Republic, Haiti and Jamaica. Without his attention directed on her, Mischief relaxed. Xander asked, "And you didn't contact Sharkey?" Her nose flushed hot pink. Ahah, just as he suspected, she was behind this. But why?

She put her paw over her eyes, as if the morning light hurt, and sneezed a fourth time. "I needed to send her the address." Her meow was so mournful that Ginny twisted around, leaned over the seat and gave her a worried look.

Xander put his chin on his paws and stared at Mischief. It would be nice to see Sharkey. She was a lovely little black and white cat, who had the potential to become a great Purrtector, but why had Mischief waited until now to mention her visit? Just what was this little apprentice of his up to? And how or why had she involved Sharkey? Worse, would he have time to catch up with her as well as conduct his investigation during the course of Mischief's supposed illness? Doubtful, but he would try.

Mischief's nose flushed red as her collar and she started to nervously snicker, but she quickly covered it with her paw as she gave another loud sneeze.

In the past two months, he'd learned that the more pitiful she looked, the more she was hiding. What was she holding back? He could tell by her body-language that it was something big and she was feeling very pleased about it. What really put a bend in his tail was that he had discovered that no matter how hard he pushed her, he couldn't find out what she was hiding until she wanted him to know. Granted, in some ways that was a good attribute for a potential Purrtector to have, but for someone trying to train her, it was a major annoyance.

As the vehicle slowed, Xander sat up to look out the window. He recognized Purrsey's home as well as the big-wheeled gray truck parked in the driveway. Squinting, he saw Rufus trimming a shrub. "Looks like your mom made good on her word and gave Rufus work."

"Why wouldn't she?" Xander knew she wanted to hop up and demand to know why he would dare suggest that someone as honorable as her mother, who was Haiti's Purrtector, would do something other than honor her word. To her credit, she did not give into temptation and kept up her sick-act.

"I knew she would," Xander clarified. "I just expected Rufus to find something else and /or for your mom to find a long-term situation for him elsewhere."

"Oh."

The rental car turned into the driveway and parked next to Rufus' big gray truck. When Mike reached into the back seat for Mischief's carry-cage, Xander took the opportunity to hop out of the car and greet Rufus. The lumbering hairy-legged man's face broke into a huge smile, as he bent down to pet him. "I heard about the little one."

Xander's ear twitched. "She'll be fine." He glanced around to make sure no one else was close enough to hear. "Actually, she is fine, she's pretending to feel ill, to give us an excuse to come here."

The big man ran a hand through his shaggy brown hair. "Wouldn't your humans bring her for a visit, if she just asked nice?"

"I'm sure they would, but there are some lingering questions about the situation we had." He tilted his head toward the Northeast. "I need to go up there and verify that things are resolved. Ms. Mischief's health is merely a diversion for my staff and any others who might be monitoring my movements."

"Oh, Ms. Sharkey told me about that, but I didn't realize the little miss's illness was part of that... When do we leave?"

We? What all had Sharkey told Rufus and how in the world did she know him? What was even more disconcerting was knowing she has discussed his business with someone else, when he hadn't even told her the details of his idea? How dare she! "I planned to grab the next bus. Do you know when that is expected?"

Rufus scooped him up and knuckle-rubbed the top of his head. "Silly cat. No reason to wait for the bus. I'll drive us direct."

This was almost too good to be true. "Thanks!"

"You sure you don't want to at least say hello to Ms. Purrsey and Ms.

Sharkey? They are good cats and Ms. Sharkey came an awful long way to see you."

"You're right, tomorrow would probably be better," Xander said. With no further encouragement, Rufus tucked him under his arm, much the way he'd seen NFL players tuck the football to run, then Rufus lumbered toward the porch.

Xander told himself the indignity was worth it in exchange for a truck ride, instead of relying on the country's questionable bus system. As if in response to his thought, a diesel-engine with an iffy muffler wheezed up the hill. Xander looked back at the road in time to see the garish colors of a bus as it passed by, leaving a thin trail of black exhaust. He wrinkled his nose. While it was obvious that several artists has spent hours making the bus unique, he wondered if humans really thought that painting bright orange and red fish scales and cartoons on buses was more important that making sure the engine was well maintained.

Rufus opened the door and stepped onto the cool, dim foyer's tile floor.

"It's about time you came in," a familiar voice said.

"Sharkey! I'm happy to see you." How had she gotten here so quickly? His tail twitched with the suspicion that Sharkey had heard of the planned diversion much earlier than Mischief had indicated.

"He who would do great things should not attempt them all alone. That's a Seneca proverb."

"Ah, Sharkey, I've missed your quotes." Rufus put him down so they could properly greet each other, with cheek rubs. "I heard you graduated with honors. Congratulations."

"Thank you." She tilted her head toward the salon, where the humans were talking about Mischief. "The kid is a good actress. If I hadn't known the plan, I would have believed she was sick, too."

Knowing the way Mischief could ham it up for photos, Xander had never doubted her acting abilities. "So how long are you here for?"

"Until we head East."

"Beg pardon?"

"Didn't anyone tell you that I'm going to Étang Saumâtre and Jimaní with you?"

"No." Xander frowned. "Why?"

Sharkey's black and white face puckered and her nose began to redden. "Council directive."

Wow, that was big! Normally, the Council only intervened with top-ranked Purrtectors, who were involved in very delicate situations. Of course, they could also give direct guidance to someone like Purrsey, who was Haiti's Purrtector, even if Haiti was a tiny country. Or perhaps Lucy Fur... Ahhh, that was probably why they had temporarily assigned Sharkey to assist. Usually, they gave him directives for operations, because, as Sea Purrtector, his jurisdiction covered about seventy-five-percent of the world and touched most of the other primary Purrtectorates in some way... Ahhhh, that must be it. The Council had contacted her because of him and his investigation, which was actually quite a compliment to him, and also a way to say the Moreau situation was urgent.

But why hadn't they let him know the plan? Something about that oversight bothered him.

It really bothered him to know that Mischief probably knew all about this, and might even have had a paw in requesting Sharkey's presence... but why?

The how was blatantly obvious. He made a mental note to change his passwords just as soon as he returned to Whispurring Winds.

"Good to have you along." Xander smiled. It was odd to see Sharkey alone. At the academy, she and her best friend, Mouse, a grayish Chihuahua, who was Catamondo's first dog trainee, had always been together. "How is Mouse?"

"He's well. After he got things sorted out in Port Antonia, Sir Simon asked him to return to Kingston. He thinks Mouse's assistance is 'invaluable help for achieving peace', and making our treaty with Dogdom work." She blinked rapidly. "We'd hoped to get posted together, but obviously, that didn't happen."

"Never say never."

Her golden eyes got huge. "Do you think it's possible? I mean, he's my best friend, ever."

Xander flicked a whisker. "Dame Esmeralda thinks Mouse is great, I'm sure that if he asked, she would know which ears to whispurr into." While he would never question the sanity or judgement of the Purrsident's littermate, and even though he had learned to like Mouse, who was the first canine to graduate from any of Catamondo's academies, in truth, he still wasn't one-hundred-percent sold on the idea of treating dogs equally. He scratched his ear and reminded himself that as a Purrtector, he needed to bury purrsonal opinions and enforce Catamondo legislation without question. In short, he needed to find a way to help cats have a good life... And, due to the peace treaty with Dogdom, he also would help decent dogs, or sort-of-dogs, like Rufus, who had been an actual dog before Dr. Moreau added some of her own DNA to Rufus' and made him something halfway between human and dog.

"But they're sending me to Puerto Rico!" Sharkey mewed. He tilted his head and stared at her until her nose blushed scarlet and she dropped her head. "Sorry," she told her toes. "You don't even have a country to call your own. I should be grateful."

Since it seemed complicated to explain that his dear Whispurring Winds was US Documented, and therefore he was sailing aboard a tiny piece of the USA, he focused on her emotional issue. "I'm sure they want the best for you. Mouse, too," he added, even though he was not certain how Catamondo actually felt about their first non-cat graduate, not to mention know what they planned to do with him, other than have him help Sir Simon achieve peace in Jamaica.

"When you know who you are; when your mission is clear and you burn with the inner fire of unbreakable will; no cold can touch your heart; no deluge can dampen your purpose. You know that you are alive," Sharkey said. "Chief Seattle of the Duwamish said that."

"Er, right," Xander said, as he accepted the fact that her odd obsession with American Indian quotes was still alive and well. He gave his head a shake. Right now, he needed to focus on his objective and tie up all questions and potential loose ends from the Moreau situation. "Will you be ready to head up to the border, tomorrow at first light?" That would give him time to make sure Mischief was doing her part, but not to the point of needing surgery or any other vile thing human medicine occasionally came up with.

"Of course." Sharkey smiled. "Rufus already asked for a few days off." She looked at him, her eyes filled with sympathy. "The poor guy wants this settled as much as we do."

Xander bit his lower lip. How much had the dog-man been told? He hadn't spared a moment to think how this mess would affect Rufus, or how the doctor had changed Rufus' situation in such an unexpected and invasive way. Was the result good or bad? Rufus had a secure position with Purrsey and she apparently had a devoted chauffeur/gardener, who had spent his life being submissive to cats and not asking why. However, that didn't mean he was happy. Was he happy, now? Had he been happy as a real dog? Xander sighed as he acknowledged he'd probably never know and wouldn't have been able to purrtect him from the scientific experiment that had transformed him from a normal dog to something strangely human, even if he'd known him back then.

Rufus and Sharkey had obviously discussed his operation and decided how and when they wanted to conduct it without giving him a say in the matter... he would never have treated another cat that way, unless they were either very young or too sick to make the choice for themselves.

He suspected that they assumed Mischief had contacted them with his blessing, instead of deciding to put her paws in his business and make plans within and around his plan. Since he didn't want to deal with this troubling aspect, Xander gave Rufus, who was now in the kitchen, a significant look. "Do you know if he likes it here?"

Sharkey's eyes gleamed. "Very." She stood up and took a step toward the living room. "He thinks Ms. Purrsey is wonderful, but Garfield is a lazy pig." She snickered. "I think he's got them pegged." She leaned close and whispurred, "Do you know that Garfield eats here AND at his own home?" A quick glance assured her no one was looking their direction. "It's no wonder he's round enough to roll!"

"Still, he is a nice tom. Not Purrtector material, but that isn't for everyone."

"Mouse's dream is to become a Purrtector."

Xander blinked hard at the idea of a Chihuahua rising to that rank, and while he didn't think it would actually be possible, he didn't know what the Council would do. Did the rules say Purrtectors needed to be cats? He'd have to check that out. Swishing his tail, he asked, "What about you? What do you dream of?"

She blushed, looked down and softly told her toes, "Having a home of my own... and maybe be a Purrtector, but just a local one, so I could have time for a family."

He nodded in understanding. Over the years, he had met a lot of cats who had basically raised themselves in the wild, so he understood why home and family were the thing she desired the most. "I'm sure you'll find what you're looking for."

"Really?" She peeked up at him, her expression hopeful.

He nodded. "I am certain you will eventually find the purrfect forever home... But first, we need to make sure my poor, sick apprentice is getting the help she needs."

"Absolutely!" Side by side, they strolled into the salon, where the veterinarian was checking Mischief's heartbeat, while Ginny wrung her hands and told him how dear little Mischief loved water and how she had been sneezing and how worried she was. Xander closed his eyes, as he listened to Ginny's distressed tone. Should he have chosen a different distraction? Something which wouldn't have caused his dear chef such stress?

Could-of, should-of, would-of... it was immaterial and the plan was already in motion, so the only thing to do was make the best of it and hope dear Ginny would relax when Mischief was recovering at the veterinarian's home.

The following morning, Xander, Sharkey and Rufus left immediately after an early breakfast. The trip to Isla Moreau, which was the late Doctor Moreau's property and located on Étang Saumâtre, was comfortable and uneventful, which only proved how horrible Haiti's bus system was by comparison. As they passed an area with smooth, glistening mud, he recalled his first trip to investigate Damon Moreau, when the bus he'd been riding on had been sucked into the horrid mud. Xander shivered at the memory.

As Rufus parked the truck by the late doctor's white clapboard house, he wondered why the lawn looked freshly mown. He put his paws on the dashboard, so he could look to where the drying shed had been, but it didn't look like anything was being maintained there. In fact, weeds and grass were so overgrown that the path from the house to the drying shed was barely noticeable. No one had begun clearing away the charred timbers or metal roofing, either. That was simultaneously good and bad. Good that evidence in the laboratory, which had been hidden in the basement under the drying shed was probably untouched; bad that the evidence was left as is and that probably meant lots of nasty smells from the rotting things and possibly even dangerous because of the spilled chemicals and germs and whatever Hathor-awful stuff the insane doctor had stored in her workplace.

Xander swallowed and told himself all would be well, but he couldn't quite believe it.

"Oh, it's beautiful here!" Sharkey said. "And so much cooler than the city." When Rufus opened the door, she hopped out and immediately began sniffing the grass. "This smells like Jamaica." She threw herself down and began to roll.

"It's grass," Xander said. "Cut fescue smells the same, everywhere."

"Don't be a sour puss." Xander felt the fur on his tail stand on end, so quickly hopped out of the truck and sat down before she had a chance to realize that she had gotten to him. Sharkey finished rolling and lay on her tummy, nose deep in the cut grass. "Don't you miss this?"

"Miss what?"

"Grass! Plants!" She rolled on her side and looked at him. "Isn't that the worst thing about living on a boat? No grass to roll in?"

"Well, since I've never rolled in grass, I wouldn't know."

She scrambled to sit up. "Seriously?" He nodded, surprised that she would think this was common. "Oh, wow! You need to try it."

"Not right now." He looked around. "Where did Rufus go?"

Startled, she looked around. "I don't know, but they were here just a second ago."

"They?" Sharkey's golden eyes widened until he saw the white rims and her nose paled. Xander controlled his breathing and glared at her. "Don't you mean he?"

The shake of her head was almost as imperceptible as her whispurred, "They." Xander continued pinning her with his glare. She licked her lips, then added, "Grown men can learn from very little children for the hearts of the little children are pure. Therefore, the Great Spirit may show to them many things which older people miss. Black Elk of the Oglala Lakota Sioux said that... Smart, wasn't he?"

"They?" Xander repeated, without blinking, but he was sure he knew what she was trying to hide. "By any chance did you and Rufus collaborate in a conspiracy to assist my willful apprentice in disobeying me?"

"You do NOT have the right to tell me what to do!" an all-too-familiar voice mewed.

He whirled to face the disobedient brat. "Don't I?" The temptation to smack her was strong, but he was older, wiser and smarter than she was – no matter what she thought. Mischief was supposed to be at the veterinarian's, acting as a diversion, not standing next to the biggest, fattest white and black rat he had ever seen. He moved into an attack stance. The homely thing was easily as big as Mischief was, but it was scared, as if a veteran of many fights. Judging by its size it was probably safe to assume that the fights had been over food and it had won. The good thing was that it was standing beside Mischief as if it were a friend, instead of a predator, who planned to eat her.

The rat cringed and moved behind Mischief, as if seeking purrtection. Mischief's leaf-green eyes sparked with anger. "You're scaring poor Scar." She took a step forward, which would have been menacing, if she was bigger. "How dare you act mean to my friend?"

"Friend?" he echoed.

"Yes, friend." She stepped closer. "He is Rufus' friend, too. In fact, they are... " She frowned, as if searching for the word.

"Taxa," the rat said.

"Taxas!" Mischief concluded.

So, the rat was some sort of genetic relative, not just a friend. "Taxon is singular, taxa is the plural," Xander said through clenched jaws.

The rat's ears and eyes appeared over Mischief's back. "He's correct," the rodent said. When Xander's posture relaxed, the creature added, "Taxa are a group of organisms linked by common ancestry."

Xander contemplated the confusing relationships Dr. Moreau had made when she'd mixed the DNA of various animals to form new creatures during her strange and often evil experiments. His gaze narrowed on the rat. "So, you're not just Rufus' friend, you're a relative."

The rat eagerly nodded as he moved back to stand by Mischief.

Xander turned his attention on Mischief. "Do you know how much trouble you've caused with your disappearing act?"

"For who?"

"Everyone, me, your mom, Mike and Ginny. The vet."

She snorted. "They won't notice."

"Yes, they will."

"NO," she shouted, then paused to control herself and added, "They won't."

"Why are you so sure about that?"

"Because Rascal is pretending to be me."

Xander's eyes threatened to cross. "And you think you can get away with that?"

"We did when we were little."

Dear Hathor, what had he been thinking when he decided an apprentice would be a good idea? "Okay, let's think this through. Even if Rascal manages to convince everyone she is you, don't you think her forever family will miss her?"

"Well, that's kinda the idea." He perked his ears and raised his brows, silently urging her to explain. "Did you know that Rascal and Dickens went to the same forever home?"

"No."

"Well, they did and they don't get along any better now than they did when we were little. She needs a break and well, when I told her about your plan, she said she wished she could take a nice peaceful break like that." Mischief attempted to twirl her whiskers. "And since I wanted to be here, we decided that we could both get what we wanted."

He was getting a headache trying to remember if Mischief and Rascal looked enough alike to fool Mike and Ginny. While he recalled that their coloring was the same and they were about the same size, their purrsonalities were totally different. Where Mischief was quiet, he recalled that Rascal had been bold and loud. Or had that just been when she argued with Dickens? He frowned and wondered if Rascal liked water and was diligent about her schoolwork. Had he chosen the wrong apprentice?

Mischief's eyes narrowed. "What are you thinking about?"

"Nothing," he said too quickly. The rat's scared face moved back and forth between them, as if he was watching a ping pong match, but he seemed to have lost his fear.

"You worry too much," Mischief growled. "This will work and everyone will be happy."

"I hope you're correct." He forced himself to relax. "Are you going to introduce me to your 'friend' or do I call him Taxon?"

"My name is Scar."

Xander inclined his head in acknowledgement of just how fitting that name was, since the fat creature had what looked like a vicious scar across his right cheek and several others over his body. During his year on Catamondo's kick-boxing circuit, he'd purrfected hooks and kicks, which could leave a similar mark on an opponent's face, but his always had at least three cuts, not one. "Good to meet you, Scar." He glanced around. "Is it just you and Rufus, or did more of your family survive?"

"We'd really like to know the answer to that question, which is why we volunteered to come."

"Understood." Xander nodded, but wondered exactly why Scar and Rufus were interested. Even more worrisome, did their allegiance lie with their taxa, whose goal was control over Catamondo? Or did they want to know they were free to build a new life on their own terms? Xander turned his attention to his willful apprentice. "Any more surprises?" She suddenly found her toes very interesting, which was a sure sign of guilt. He sighed. "Out with it."

"Mr. Mars came, too," she whispurred to her toes. Xander felt his whiskers perk in anticipation of seeing the lisping chameleon, who was one of the best spies he had ever met, but he didn't see him anywhere. Mischief raised her head enough to peek at him. "Ms. Sharkey doesn't know about him and he's afraid of her."

"Why?"

"When she first arrived, she said that iguana tasted like chicken."

"I've heard that's true."

"Well, what if she mistakes him for an iguana and eats him?" she asked. Scar solemnly nodded.

"I can see why he could be concerned, but I will be happy to assure her that he is a trusted ally and not to be nibbled on."

Mischief raised her head, her cheerful disposition returned. Xander scratched his ear and wondered how to teach her to behave, then, a worse thought brought him up short: her way wasn't necessarily bad. In fact, in many ways, her plan was better than his, because he didn't need to shoulder all the problems and could share the investigation with Sharkey and Mars, who he trusted. He wished he could trust Mischief, but she was a bit too young and naive. Worse, she had apparently told several others what his plan was. He could only hope that she hadn't mentioned anything when the catarazzi, who liked to spy on him, were within earshot. While it was wonderful to be able to ride all the way in an air conditioned vehicle, which didn't get mired in mud, where did Rufus' and Scar's allegiance lie? While Rufus had helped save him during the fire and had taken the position with Purrsey, had he had second thoughts? And was his true allegiance to Purrsey or his taxa and their sinister plans? Had he taken the position with Purrsey so he could spy for his family?

And when had Scar come into the picture? Had he been here all the time? Since Mischief seemed to have met him, previously, Xander suspected Scar had somehow tracked Rufus down, but how could he ask without alerting the rodent about his doubts regarding his loyalty and motives?

And where was Rufus?

For that matter, where was Sharkey?

He studied Mischief, who was now standing shoulder to shoulder with a rat; he had a bad feeling about this new friendship she seemed to have made. Worse, he suspected that she might be in the middle of a conspiracy to undermine him. The problem was that he didn't know who to trust and what everyone's agenda was.

His own agenda was clear: he needed to verify that the Moreau situation was no longer a threat to Catamondo and determine Lucy Fur's involvement. Furthermore, he needed to find out why Ms. Fur had disappeared from the headlines. When the fur on his back threatened to stand on end, Xander willed himself to relax. Until he had enough information to sort fact from imagination, he needed to watch and listen. It was possible that everything was fine, but his intuition told him that it was not.

"Lunch!" Sharkey called, from the porch.

Ah, so that's where the others had disappeared to. He motioned for Mischief and Scar to precede him. As they walked through the freshly cut grass, he wondered, again, who was taking care of this place – and why. Even more baffling: when and where had Mischief met Scar? For certain, they had not just met when they arrived. And she hadn't met him aboard Whispurring Winds – he would have noticed the distinctive rodent aroma. He frowned as he walked up the steps to the porch. There hadn't been any scent of rat at Purrsey's home, either. So where had his headstrong apprentice met the rat? And why did they act like friends?

As they entered through the pet door, Xander recalled that the rat had also seemed to know Mars, so the rodent must have been at Purrsey's home. It was the only explanation for how he could know both Mischief and Mars. Wasn't it?

Xander batted his collar and turned on its recording feature. While things were not bad enough – yet – for him to have it creating a full backup of his activities in his cloud storage, he didn't know who he could trust and in case he did not survive, he needed to leave some sort of record documenting events.

While he wanted to trust Sharkey, her best friend was a Chihuahua. Could a reliable cat have a dog for a best friend? He winced as he thought of several cats that did. It was probably wise not to judge her on the basis of one strange relationship.

He looked around the dusty house. A spider had built a big web in one doorway and he smelled rodent. Unlike the yard, it didn't appear to have been lived in or cared for in a while. He followed the rat – he reminded himself to think of him as Scar, at least until he knew for a fact that he was not an ally – into the kitchen. This room didn't smell stale, like the front hallway: it looked clean and smelled of canned tuna. Rufus was busy setting five dishes on the table, where Sharkey was already seated. Fortunately, she knew her manners, so had not begun eating. Xander hopped onto the chair next to her and sniffed the tuna. Since moving aboard Whispurring Winds, Mike had been able to indulge his love of fishing, so they frequently dined on fresh sea food. Until now, he hadn't realized how different canned was from fresh. He glanced out the window and wished it wouldn't be rude to begin his investigation, instead of being sociable and eating.

When everyone was seated, Rufus motioned for them to eat.

Since it was the politically correct thing to do, Xander ate. He also glanced around, wondering where Mars was, or if Mischief had simply been living up to her name when she mentioned him. He had almost convinced himself that his disobedient apprentice had lied to him, when he noticed a pair of familiar brown eyes just above Rufus' shirt pocket. Narrowing his gaze, he saw that Mars, who was apparently inside the pocket, except for his front paws and head, had managed to perfectly match the taupe color of Rufus' shirt. The chameleon was getting good with this color changing. In fact, the only way he could have hidden better was if he could change the color of his eyes.

How nice it must be to simply disappear by altering the color of one's fur or skin. Just as quickly as he formed the idea, he discarded it. His seal-point coat was purrfect, as it was, and purrfection should never be dyed.

Mars noticed that he'd been spotted and gave an exaggerated look of worry at Sharkey. Strange that he wasn't worried about the rat – er, Scar – as far as he knew, rats ate anything that didn't eat them, first.

"Humankind has not woven the web of life. We are but one thread within it. Whatever we do to the web, we do to ourselves. All things are bound together. All things connect. Chief Seattle said that." Sharkey turned to Xander and asked. "The Duwamish are smart, aren't they?"

Xander swallowed his mouthful of tuna, and wondered if the Duwamish were an American Indian tribe. Knowing Sharkey, it was the most likely guess. And probably Chief Seattle was their leader. Dare he assume the tribe was from Merlin's Purrtectorate? That was the only Seattle he knew of, but was it the only one? With a quick flick of his claw, he activated his collar's information archive and thought 'Duwamish'. Native American tribe in western Washington, and the indigenous people of metropolitan Seattle, where they have been living since the end of the last glacial period was the response. It was gratifying to know his suspicions were spot on. Xander smiled at Sharkey. "I liked the Puget Sound area when I visited and think people were smart to move there."

Sharkey gave him a disgruntled look. "What does the Puget Sound have to do with things connecting?"

"Just commenting on the Duwamish." Xander gently batted her ear. "Was there something in particular you wanted to point out with your quotation?" She wasn't thinking about that spider web in the hallway, was she?

She motioned around the table. "We're all here, each for our own reason, but all of us have the same goal. I think that is a great connection. Don't you?"

Did they really have the same goal? He'd like to think so, but had doubts. "Why are you here?" He tilted his head. "I mean, I understand why resolving this is important to the others. Rufus and Scar need closure, so they can plan their futures. Mischief, Mars and I want to assure what we began was properly finished... but do you have a connection other than your directive?"

Sharkey clamped her jaws together and glared at him, then got a strange look that made her ears flatten. "Mars?" She looked around the table, her gaze abruptly stopping on Rufus' chest, where Mars was blushing over all the attention. Whiskers stiff, she stared at the chameleon. "Can I assume you are Mars?" He nodded. "And your involvement and interest in getting this situation resolved for Catamondo is not questioned, while mine is?" By the time she was finished with her question, her fur was standing on end. Mars paled, then dove into Rufus's pocket to hide.

"You shouldn't act mean to your friends," Rufus told Sharkey.

"Friends?" Her voice rose an octave. Xander instinctively moved into attack mode, and prepared to tackle Sharkey if she made a move toward the pocket Mars was hiding in.

"Yes, friends," Rufus growled.

Sharkey sprang to her paws, fur flared and eyes blazing gold fire.

Xander gently head butted her. "He is my friend."

"He is a chameleon!"

Xander snorted. "This from the cat whose best friend is a Chihuahua.... a cat who just reminded everyone that each of us is a woven thread of the same life?" Her fur trembled and her mouth dropped open. Mars' eyes appeared above the rim of the pocket, but Xander kept his attention on Sharkey. "Do not judge others for their relationships if you don't want others to judge you. I gave Mouse the benefit of the doubt and learned he had honorable traits, so while I don't consider him my best friend, I can see why you value him. Now, please take my word for it that Mars is a good fellow and he is one of the best spies I have ever met. I don't know if we'll need someone for covert infiltration or not, but if we do, we are lucky he volunteered."

The only way Sharkey could have studied him more closely was if she'd put him under a microscope. He waited patiently for her to think it through. When she did, she sighed, "Fine, the lizard is a friend."

Around the table, breaths that had been held were released, Mars yelped, "Iss as chameleons!"

Xander leaned so close that only Sharkey could hear, and as he made a show of rubbing cheeks, whispurred, "Don't let the lisp fool you, he is actually quite smart." In a normal tone, he added, "I'm glad you understand that he is as valuable to this mission as you are."

Her eyes widened, but that was her only reaction. Turning to Rufus, she stared at his pocket, "You can come out. I won't hurt you."

"Iss rights heres," Mars said, then altered his color enough for her to see him sitting on Rufus' shoulder.

Sharkey blinked. "I see why Xander thinks you are so valuable. That is an amazing skill."

"Well, Ms. Sharkey, I guess you is all right, too," Rufus said.

Her nose turned red at the compliment, and for once, she didn't address her toes, as she gave him a pretty thank you.

Xander returned to eating the canned tuna and evaluated which items on his 'to do list' were most important. Then, as he finished, he turned to Scar and asked, "Do you know how many of your other taxa are still alive?"

The rat shook his head.

Xander controlled his frustration and tried to remain friendly. "It's lucky you weren't in the lab when it caught fire."

"But I was!" Scar exclaimed. "I've never been so afraid in all my life and that includes all the times Doc M knocked me out to get more DNA samples."

"You were there?" Mischief's eyes were huge. "How come you never said so?"

Xander's claws sank into the chair seat as he wondered how many others had escaped the fire... this was starting to look a lot more complicated than he had expected.

"You never asked," Scar told Mischief. "But yes, I'd gone down there for dinner, then stayed to find out what the big meeting was about."

Xander's ears perked. "What did you find out?"

Scar snorted. "Nothing. You should know that, since you were the one that disrupted everything before it began." Mars nodded in agreement.

"I thought so, but wasn't sure," Xander admitted, then asked a question he'd wondered and worried about, "Where was Damon?"

Scar and Rufus looked at each other, then the dog-man shrugged and Scar said, "I don't know and I worry about that. He is evil, always telling me he gonna eat me if I don't do exactly what he wants, when he wants."

"When was the last time you saw him?"

A frown furrowed Scar's fat face. "When he came back from the Festival." Scar looked at Rufus, who again shrugged, then nodded in agreement.

"Was that common?" Xander asked.

"Pretty much," Scar said. "He was a big shot when the taxa had a meeting, but I never saw much of him otherwise."

Rufus let out a bark of laughter, "That's 'cause you avoided him."

"And for good reason." Scar glared at Rufus, "He bit you when he thought you didn't move fast enough, too." His long bare tail lashed back and forth with tension.

Xander gave Scar's scars a closer look and realized some could be bite marks. What sort of family-unit had those taxa been? In an effort to continue gathering information, instead of let the conversation devolve into emotion, Xander asked, "Since you survived the fire, do you think there is a chance the doctor, Chester, Matsu or Mingus did?"

"I know they didn't get out the way I did," Scar said. When Xander raised a brow, he added, "They were too big to fit in the utility conduit I escaped through. In fact, I was lucky not to get stuck."

"What about Clade and Allele?" Rufus asked. "Did you see if they got out?"

Scar shook his head so hard his jowls jiggled. "They might have though, through one of the Vi-Purrs' tunnels."

A chill passed over Xander. "Tunnels?"

Rufus nodded.

Mischief and Mars looked at each other, eyes huge.

Sharkey looked from one to the other, obviously confused. A big boom shook the house. Xander jumped and every strand of fur was standing on end before his paws reconnected with his seat, but no one else noticed because they had all had similar reactions. In fact, Mars had fallen off Rufus' shoulder.

"What was that?" Mischief meowed.

"Thunder – at least I think it was thunder," Rufus said, then he bent down to pick up Mars.

Where there was thunder, there was lightning and that could mess up his collar, so Xander turned it off.

"Thunder, like with rain?" Mischief's terror instantly transformed to excitement. "Ginny hardly ever lets me play in the rain!" With a leap and a bounce she was dashing toward the door.

"What's with her?" Sharkey asked.

"A very unnatural obsession with water," Xander said. Strange that the things he tried to avoid in a storm were the same things that Mischief wanted to experience. Play in a storm? He shivered at the idea.

"Seriously?" Sharkey said.

He nodded. "If she doesn't watch it, she's going to get herself sick for real."

"Or electrocuted," Sharkey meowed. "Aren't you going to go save her from herself?"

"And deprive her of the consequences of her choices?" Xander shook his head. "She doesn't seem to learn when I tell her, so I'm trying to find out if she can learn from her mistakes."

"Children learn from what they see. We need to set an example of truth and action."

"Who said that?"

"Howard Rainer. He is with the tribe at Taos Pueblo-Creek."

Aha, he thought so. Ignoring the thunder, which kept getting closer, Xander turned his attention on Scar and Rufus, intent upon finding out as much as possible about Isla Moreau and the creatures – he hesitated to think of them as cats – who might still be alive and plotting against Catamondo.

Chapter 3

"I've never actually been down here, before," Scar admitted, as he peered into a dusty rough-cut tunnel that branched off the equally grimy one they were in.

"And you never thought to mention that before now?" Xander asked, as he pawed a sticky cobweb off his ear, and watched the displaced spider flee down the side passageway. He ended up with bits of the nasty web clinging to his ear, whiskers and paw. Yuck! The things he was forced to endure for the honor of Catamondo. He sniffed the air, which was foul, but also stale, so he didn't think anything – with the exception of the spider, whose home he'd just ruined – had been down here in a long time.

Was there an exit, which someone or something could have escaped through? The thought of Chester, Mingus, Matsu, or the doctor who had created them, escaping made his fur want to stand on end, but what really worried him was the possibility that Clade and Allele, the odd cat-snake mix might have survived. What if they had joined Damon while he was babysitting little Miss Water Nymph? Xander wanted to spit at the thought. Damon plus those Vi-Purrs would be a dreadful combination to deal with. The worst thing was that he didn't have a clue exactly what the Vi-Purrs might be capable of. Xander pushed aside his dark thoughts and asked, "What can you tell me about Clade and Allele?"

"They like to bite." Scar rubbed the scar on his face.

"Are they poisonous?"

"They can be." Scar glanced back at him. "They have snake DNA along with macaw woven into their cat strand." Xander wasn't surprised to hear that. "And, like snakes, they learned how to control how much venom they inject."

"I've heard that baby snakes are more dangerous than the adults because they don't know how to do that."

Scar nodded. "Doc M had to lock them up for months until they learned control."

"You were there?"

"Of course," Scar snorted, "I was one of her original lab projects."

"So that's why you look so normal."

Scar laughed. "You think that because I referred to them as taxa I'm one of the doc's mutants." He shook his head. "Sorry, but I'm a genuine lab rat. I refer to them as my taxa because she included some of my DNA in the first strands. Some of her own, too, but mainly in her alternations to Rufus." He flicked his whip-like tail. "I don't think she liked how he looked, or the knowledge that he was part of her." His tail whipped harder. "But that didn't stop her from taking what she wanted from me or poor old Gabby."

"Gabby?"

"The macaw she used to have as a pet. She liked the idea of using some of Gabby's DNA to give her creations longer life. In fact, she tapped poor ole Gabby so often that the wretched bird up and died."

Well, that explained why Chester, Mingus and Matsu's fur looked more like long, thin feathers instead of normal fur. "She used Gabby's DNA for Clade and Allele, too, didn't she?"

"Yes." Scar stopped to sniff a crack in the wall. "She often told Rufus that he was her very own Sasquatch and now she had made chupacabras." He snorted. "She can call them chupacabras all she wants and try to scare people, but Rufus and I always called them Vi-Purrs 'cause they're mostly snake and cat." He stopped walking and looked at the wall, then stepped closer, until his nose nearly touched it. "Hmm. This is interesting."

Xander's ears perked and he moved forward to see what had caught the rat's interest. Unlike a natural crack, this one appeared very straight. Since he had excellent vision in the dark, he could see enough to know Scar was on to something, but not enough to figure out exactly what he was looking at, so he quickly keyed his collar to analyze what appeared to be a natural rock wall... but wasn't.

Why would they need to hide something when the Vi-Purrs were the only ones who came down here? "Are you sure that Clade and Allele are the ones who dug these tunnels?"

"They claimed to, but I know they lie, so your guess is as good as mine." Scar nudged a spot near the strange crack and a portion of the wall pivoted, like an opening door. "Thought so," Scar said with satisfaction. He pushed again, harder, this time, and the crack enlarged enough for them to see there was a room on the other side. Scar paused, whiskers quivering, seemingly afraid to enter. Since Xander figured the rat knew Clade and Allele's habits better than he did, he was happy to wait. Scar sniffed the air for a long time, then cautiously entered the space.

Xander counted to ten before following.

"Just as I suspected," Scar said. "They must have come down here to escape the fire, then stayed a while, but near as I can tell, they left a while ago."

"You can tell that by smell?"

Scar flicked his tail toward some crumbs. "That and their notes." Indeed, the rodent appeared to be reading scratchy writing in a notebook. "I knew they detested Lucy, but didn't know how much."

"What do you mean?"

Scar tapped the notebook with a grimy claw. "They decided that Lucy was responsible for you coming here and ruining their plan, so they blame her and want to get even."

"How did they come to that conclusion?"

"Simple. She's a Purrtector. You're a Purrtector that helps other Purrtectors. Plus she met with Damon, Mat and Ming about the same time you showed up... Can't you see why they decided that Lucy hadn't just set off on her own, but changed sides, so she was against them?" Xander stared at the fat rat. Scar glared back. "It isn't rocket science."

"Purrhaps not, but my arrival had nothing to do with Miss Fur. In fact, until you confirmed her identity, I wasn't positive that she was the one I observed meeting them at the lake."

Scar blinked. "Then why were you here?"

"Ms. Purrsey Lourdes requested my help. My investigation led me here."

"You were investigating?" Xander nodded. "What?"

"Catnip riots and the murders that began in Port-au-Prince after our peace treaty with Dogdom... fears about chupacabras," Xander said. "I have only heard about one chupacabra confirmed attack, plus there have been some sightings of strange animals about the size of a pig since the fire." He shrugged. "I suspect that your Vi-Purrs might have been the cause of the chupacabra reports."

Scar frowned. "They must be keeping a low profile until they figure out a new plan – one that doesn't involve Lucy and the others."

"What was their original plan?" Xander asked.

Scar gave him an odd look. "I thought you'd figured that out and that's why you originally came here... they wanted to take over Catamondo by creating a clone from the Purrsident's DNA... they were making one from yours too – figured they could claim it was you, even though when they started, they thought you was just some wharf cat and they knew that they could control the clones, which meant they could control Catamondo."

"And if they'd had a chance to create those clones, then what?"

"What do you think? If they'd grown the replacements, then they'd have taken you and Purrsident Mitzi out." Scar's tail made a slashing motion.

Xander nodded. "That's what I figured, but it helps to verify." His own tail twitched in memory of the close call he'd had when his identity had been discovered. Thank Hathor that Chester Moreau had not been able to use his fur and the fur stolen from Purrsident Mitzi Montgomery to create any clones. The very thought of being replaced by something created in a lab and controlled by someone as evil as Chester made him taste bile. "I just can't figure out why Doctor

Moreau was interested in taking over Catamondo's government."

"She wasn't."

"Explain."

"She was interested in creating scary taxa – that's why she was so disgusted with Ruf – he looked like a Sasquatch, but wasn't scary... Clade and Allele, now she thought they were excellent chupacabras and you gotta admit they look scary."

Xander remembered his first glimpse of them and the way their screeches to the morning sun had made his fur stand on end. He tried not to shiver at the mental picture of strange creatures the size of small mud-colored bears, which had a row of spines reaching from their necks to the base of their tails. Their long, pointy snouts had crocodile-like teeth. Worse, they flew on big bat-like wings. But the worst thing had been their eyes, which appeared to be mounted on top of their skulls. "I don't understand why you don't think she liked Rufus. He is nice and helpful, while Clade and Allele seem useless."

"They are destructive and they scare everyone."

"True."

"Well, don't you get it?" Xander shook his head. Scar sighed, then explained, "Doc M was mad at humans for making problems for her while she was in India, so she wanted to create creatures to scare and torture them. She started with Chester and Lucy and that didn't go so well, 'cause Lucy left and Chester didn't terrify people. Then, she went to work on Ming and Mat and while they were okay, she figured bigger would be better, and came up with Damon and Doodle -"

"Doodle? Why is this the first time I've heard of him?"

Scar shrugged. "He moved to Port-au-Prince and started the coven – you saw them arrive just before the fire." Xander's fur threatened to stand on end at the realization that there had been two black cats the size of Damon. "But all four of them aligned with Chester and decided they wanted their own agenda – taking over Catamondo."

"So Lucy Fur and Doctor Moreau weren't behind the plan?"

Scar shook his head. "Lucy left long before Chester hatched that."

"But the doctor helped them?"

He nodded. "It was the only way they would agree to help her get what she wanted."

"And that was?"

"Helping her control the Vi-Purrs, plus give her samples of their DNA to splice into her other experiments. She had a new batch ready to come out of the tanks the night of the fire. That was why the taxa had all come."

"Even Lucy?"

"No, not her. She met with Ming and Mat a day or two before, 'cause they threatened her somehow, if she didn't at least meet, but from what I heard, she basically told them she disowned them. That really pissed off Chester, her being his vat-mate and all."

"Vat mate?"

"Same DNA batch and grown in the same tank." Xander recalled the odd things in the strange aquariums and shivered. "Come to think of it, after Lucy was here, I didn't see Damon around." Scar's chubby face contorted into a frown. "I wonder if Chester sent him to talk to Lucy or if he might'a decided that if Lucy and Doodle could go it alone and do their own thing, he could, too."

"Are you saying that Damon wasn't the top cat?"

Scar gave a snort of laughter. "He was meant to seem so, but no, that was always Chester... Him and Lucy was always opposites – her loving being the center of attention and him preferring to lurk in the shadows, but both of them loved having power over others and feeling important."

"What about you?" Xander asked, "What do you like?"

"Food. And not being stuck with needles or used for tests."

They lapsed into silence as they read through the notes and looked for clues. Xander scratched his collar and tagged the audio-video file to be sent to Merlin and Fluffy. It never hurt to have a backup copy of one's research. Now, the question was if the rat had told him the truth or simply believed it was the truth based on his impressions. Only time would tell.

A loud boom shook the ground. Dust fell from the ceiling.

"Must be afternoon," Scar said. "I didn't realize we'd been down here so long."

Xander was about to question what he meant, then he recalled that during the rainy season this area generally got afternoon rain. "Does it always involve lightning?"

"Nope, just sometimes. But this is two days in a row, so I wonder if this has something to do with that tropical depression just north of us."

Tropical depression? Xander quickly checked his collar's weather feature and learned that indeed, a huge storm was slowly moving toward his location. His apprentice would probably run out and play in the rain and get herself sick for real. Indeed, his excellent hearing picked up the sound of running paws.

"Xander, are you alright?" Sharkey called.

He went to the door and called assurances back to her. But after three more booms, Sharkey and Mischief appeared in the room. He perked his ears. "I'm amazed that you came down here instead of dashing out and getting sopping wet." He was more surprised that their coats and collars looked like mottled charcoal. In fact, the only thing the proper color were their eyes.

"Ms. Sharkey says lightning kills."

"True." Both of them needed a good scrubbing to get rid of the grime and rancid stench of chemicals and death.

Mischief shuddered. "How come you never said so?"

He blinked in surprise. "I thought you knew that lightening could kill and were simply being foolhardy." She shook her head. "Well, in that case, it isn't a good idea to take refuge under a tree or by metal things because lightning likes tall things, plus metal and water conduct electricity... except a Faraday cage is metal and it's safe to be under one of those."

"What's a fair-a-day cage?"

"A Faraday cage is a sort of enclosure made by conductive material or metal mesh. It channels electricity around whatever is inside and is good purrtection from electricity."

"Like a car?" Sharkey asked. "Duchess said it was safe to be in vehicles during storms, but she thought it was because of the rubber tires."

"Yes, if the car was made of metal, I think you could consider it a sort of Faraday cage and I imagine that the tires would be good, too. But if you're in that sort of situation, make sure you don't touch the metal that's purrtecting you."

Mischief nodded solemnly. "I'll remember."

Scar peered out the door. "Where's Ruf?"

"Still sorting through stuff in the lab," Mischief said. "He said he wanted to continue looking to see if there could have been another exit, but I think he didn't want to come down here." She glanced at Sharkey. "Did you sort of feel like he was afraid to come down here?" Sharkey nodded. "That's what I thought." Mischief looked at Scar. "How come he thinks it's scary down here?"

"This was Clade and Allele's special place and they weren't very fond of Ruf," the rat said. "Actually none of the other taxa liked him because he was always trying too hard to please everyone. He still is."

"How so?" Xander asked.

"Well, even though they're all gone, he still comes up here once a week to mow the lawn and do his chores." Scar scratched his ear. "Of course, that was good for me, since I was able to ride back with him. Don't know what I'd have done otherwise." Thunder boomed, but farther away, this time. "We was pals, before, but that's when me and Ruf became best buds."

"Because the others didn't like you, either?" Mischief asked. Scar nodded. She looked around the room. "Did you find anything interesting or useful?"

"Perhaps," Xander said. "As long as you're here, you can help read these notes and journals to see if you can find a clue about if they survived the fire and if so, where they might have gone."

"Anything is better than that nasty-smelling lab!" Mischief plunked right down, causing a tiny dust cloud, then focused on a claw-written note. "What's a col-ma-do?"

"A combination of a corner store and bar," Scar said. "They're common in the mountains."

"Ah," Mischief said, then returned to reading through the stack of notes. "These seem to be about a bunch of different places. Do you really think it's worth taking the time to read them?"

Xander put aside the journal and went over to her. Looking over her shoulder, he saw Elías Piña, Jimaní, Dajabón, and Malpasse. His collar quickly confirmed they were names of towns in both Haiti and the Dominican Republic. "Good for you to recognize names of places."

"Why wouldn't I? I've lived here all my life, after all!" Her swishing tail left a trail of dust on the table. "Is it a coincidence that Tante Lucy's home is in Jimani?"

"Perhaps, but I don't like coincidences."

"Neither do I," Sharkey said.

A quick check of his collar informed Xander that Jimaní was on a main thoroughfare connecting the Dominican Republic to Haiti and there was a duty-free open-air marketplace operating on the border with the Haitian town of Malpasse. Another coincidence or clues that pointed in a specific direction? Deciding to trust his gut, Xander said, "I think that as soon as we are satisfied with our investigation here, we need to head across the border and see if we can find Miss Lucy Fur."

"In our every deliberation, we must consider the impact of our decisions on the next seven generations," Sharkey said.

Xander studied her. "Does that mean you disagree with going to Jimaní?"

"No, but I think we should be looking for those Vi-Purr things, not a Purrtector that may or may not be missing."

"Well, that's why I think Jimaní is a good place to go. I suspect that with this base destroyed, they would have headed for the closest secondary safe place."

"And that's Jimaní," Mischief concluded.

Xander nodded.

"Fine. I'm in," Sharkey said. With that, they all returned to reading.

Chapter 4

Rufus eased his gray king-cab pickup into a parking place along the street, next to the huge open-air market. There were pedestrians everywhere, all of which seemed to be dressed in the same bright colors that the buses were painted. Almost all seemed to be in a rush to either get away from where they'd been or get to wherever they were going. "Sorry, but I can't take the truck any further," Rufus said, his large brown eyes apologetic. "I don't have the proper papers to cross the border into the Dominican Republic, but you can walk right through the market."

Sharkey stared at the bustling crowd. "Do any of them know where they're going?"

"Probably not," Rufus said.

"How will we find wherever Lucy Fur lives?"

"I know the way," Scar said. "Ruf is too big to sneak over the border, but I don't have that problem."

"Have you been there, before?" Xander asked.

"Not exactly," the rat admitted. Xander perked his ears and waited expectantly. It took a bit of patience, but Scar cleared his throat, "I saw a map."

Mmmmm. Great. Xander had felt confident after studying the map of Jamaica, too, but had quickly learned that lines on a map could be very simple, yet the reality of a cross-country trip was anything but simple.

"How far away is Jimani?" Sharkey asked, and Xander suspected that she was remembering the same trip.

"It's on the other side of the market."

So was the Atlantic Ocean, but that didn't mean it was within walking distance. Xander clicked on his collar and learned, 'Jimaní is the capital and the second largest city of the Independencia Province of the Dominican Republic.' Wonderful, finding Lucy was probably going to be a lot more complicated than he thought. Why hadn't he researched Lucy's file in depth before leaving, when he had an assured way to recharge his collar's power unit, instead of assume that Rufus could drive him right to her front door, where he would presumably have another way to recharge?

"I'm really sorry," Rufus said. "I guess I should'a mentioned the paperwork thing before, but I'll stay right here and wait for you."

"Something tells me that we won't be back today. Probably not even tomorrow," Xander said.

"Oh, then maybe I should go somewhere."

"That would probably be wise." Xander scratched his ear. "If you go back to Purrsey's I could contact her when we know when we expect to be back here and then you could either come back or we could get a bus."

Rufus eagerly nodded. "Yes. That would work." His brow furrowed. "But are you sure you don't want me to wait?"

"It's probably best if you don't."

Sharkey's nod of agreement left a faint scent of soot. A close look confirmed that she still had a few charcoal smudges on her fur. If she'd shared Mischief's love of water, she would no longer smell of old fire.

Mischief looked back and forth between them, then told Rufus, "Whatever you do, do NOT tell my mom or anyone else that I'm here. Rascal really needs a break from Dickens and I want to learn how to be a good Purrtector, so I need to be here."

Rufus solemnly nodded. "I won't tell. Ever!"

"See that you don't." She gave him such a stern look that he gulped while nodding and started to choke.

A bus blaring Latino music chugged by in a haze of diesel fumes, which made them all cough, sneeze and wipe tears from their eyes.

"Let's get going," Xander said. He covertly turned on his collar's GPS feature, making sure not to accidentally scratch Mars, who had curled over his sapphire-studded collar and turned brown, which not only hid his collar from potential thieves, which he had heard were all over the market, but it also gave Mars, who had the shortest legs, a way to keep up and not run the risk of being stepped on, or get lost in the jumble.

Everyone, except Rufus, hopped out and began dodging around people, poultry and rubble, as they followed him through the confusion of the market's stalls, which didn't seem to have a pattern, since toys were displayed next to tomatoes and clothes hung on a rack with a bunch of bananas. Worse, everything stank of rotting fish and diesel, so he tried not to breathe more than enough to sustain life. The sooner he was out of this horrid market, the better.

"Oh, look!" Mischief said, as she veered off to the right. "How cool is that?"

"What are you looking at?" Scar asked, as he hurried after her.

Yes, what had she seen that could totally distract her from the mission and encourage her to run off? Did the silly kitten have a clue about the dangers of a place like the market? No sooner did he switch direction, to follow his willful apprentice, but he felt a nasty stickiness between his toes. A micro-second later, he smelled the distinctly unpleasant smell of tobacco mixed with exhaust fumes and rotting fish. He didn't need to look down to know that by changing direction, he had stepped in chewing tobacco some inconsiderate human had hawked out onto the sidewalk. What was wrong with some of the two-legs? A glance at the throng of humans confirmed that he and his friends weren't the only ones without shoes. But what really made him blink was the sight of one human heading toward the market with a big fat pig on a leash... and the pig looked happy. Didn't the fool suspect what could happen to it at a market that sold all sorts of meat – pork, ham and bacon included?

However, the pig's fate was not his problem and it was not the time to deal with the nasty mess oozing between his toes, he had to keep an eye on Mischief and save her from her own distractions.

Mischief dodged through a cat-entryway, which was set in an ancient, weathered wood door, which probably hadn't been painted in the last century. In fact, he was quite surprised to see that a modern entrance had been installed in it.

Xander paused and looked at the entryway. So did Sharkey. Scar looked from one to the other of them, as if trying to decide what to do. Xander's attention focused on a familiar logo above the faded door. It had been painted there so long ago that it was nearly indiscernible, but apparently Mischief had spotted it and decided that an office of The Daily Mews was a good place to go for information. The annoying thing was that she was correct. If anyone knew about Lucy Fur's whereabouts, as well as the possible location, or at least sightings of Damon and the others, it would be an editor or the catarazzi, which free-lanced for him or her. He glanced at Scar and wondered if rodents ever went into the Mews and suspected they didn't. Xander turned to Sharkey. "Think you can find somewhere close, but out of the way to hang out while I try to save Mischief from her whims?"

"A very great vision is needed and the man who has it must follow it as the eagle seeks the deepest blue of the sky. Crazy Horse of the Oglala Lakota Sioux said that." After that baffling statement, Sharkey and Scar headed toward a table displaying hand-woven baskets, and ducked into the shadows under it.

Xander wished there was a welcome mat to rub his poor paws on, but there wasn't and there was no benefit in procrastinating, so he hopped through the cat door and landed on a cool, bluish tile floor. It smelled of vanilla and lemons, which was a wonderful change from the actual market.

Finding Mischief amid the crowd of cats busily tapping out messages on tablets and iPhones was simple. All he needed to do was pause to listen. "My mama is Purrsey Lourdes, you know, Purrtector of Haiti."

"That's fine, Miss Mischief, but I still can't give you that information," the voice of a patient grand dame said.

Xander silently walked into the library and stood behind Mischief. The old lady's orange eyes glanced at him, then did a double-take. Having her full attention on him was disconcerting, so he returned the favor and blatantly stared into her strange eyes. The dowager's fur was tufts of black and white, which stuck out like Einstein's hair, whose photo was on the front of the biography Mike was reading. He had never seen a cat with such wild fur or bright orange eyes. Had his apprentice found another of Doctor Moreau's experiments? "Well, I never thought our Sea Purrtector would walk into my office," she said in a voice that seemed a bit too loud and rasping, yet somehow suited her.

Mischief spun around. "You followed me!"

"You didn't give me a choice, did you?" Her nose reddened. Xander narrowed his eyes at her calico face and asked, "Did you ever think that if we got separated, you not only put yourself in jeopardy, but the rest of us, as well?"

"I'm sorry." She didn't look sorry, she looked smug. "But when I saw Professor Meowingtons, and realized she was probably going into The Daily Mews' office, I guess I didn't think about us getting separated, I just thought how wonderful it was to see her and I just knew that if anyone knew where Tante Lucy was, it would be Professor Meowingtons." She gave him the big-eyed baby look, which always seemed to work on Ginny. Fortunately, he was not as easily manipulated as his chef.

Xander stepped forward and said, "So, you are Professor Meowingtons." She inclined her regal, yet alarming head. "My apprentice frequently tells me about things you taught her at The Academy."

"Unlike her brother, Master Dickens," the professor's nose wrinkled as if she was remembering a bad smell, "Miss Mischief was a good student." Mischief stood a bit straighter.

"Good to know." Xander smiled into her alarming eyes and tried not to shiver. "I assumed Mischief's classes were in Port-au-Prince." The professor inclined her head. Xander's ears instinctively started to flatten, but he forcefully perked them up, instead of allowing them to give away his annoyance with this grand dame. "So why are you here?"

Her smile showed impressive fangs and he recalled that he had heard rumors that there were vampires in this country. It wasn't easy, but his extensive training allowed him to keep his fur from standing on end. He held his ground and smiled back. She finally said, "Malpasse serves as one of the two main thoroughfares between Haiti and the Dominican Republic, and one can find out a great deal of information in the open-air market." Which, in large part, was why he was here, but it certainly didn't explain why she was. He tilted his head, silently urging her to continue. She finally added, "The town was extensively damaged in the flash flood of May 25, 2004, which killed many citizens during the night and washed away hundreds of homes." Interesting information, but about as useful as one of Sharkey's quotes. "My home was one of the ones destroyed."

"I didn't know you came from here!" Mischief said.

Professor Meowingtons inclined her scary-looking head, but her orange gaze never left Xander's face, and he continued to give her a friendly smile. "Indeed," she said. "In fact, I still come here on weekends and check into this office to make certain they don't need anything and are covering all pertinent topics." It felt like her eyes turned into lasers as they stared at him. "I find it very interesting that no one mentioned you were in this area."

"Just passing through."

"May I ask why?"

While it was not her business, particularly if she was somehow associated with The Daily Mews, if he wanted information, it was wise to give a bit. "Officially, I am aboard Whispurring Winds and anchored off Les Cayes." He leaned slightly forward and lowered his voice, in a confidential manner. "Unofficially, I am up here looking for Lucy Fur, who has not been seen in several weeks. By any chance, do you know where she might live and/or why she has been noticeably absent?"

Her eyes widened so much that they reminded him of twin harvest moons. "I am here for a similar reason."

"What's your connection with The Daily Mews?"

"Retired editor, though I am also still on the board of directors."

Ah, that explained a lot. "Is it usual for Miss Fur to vanish like this?"

"Indeed, not!"

"Just as I thought." He leaned a bit closer and dropped his voice, even further, "Yet that is not the most disturbing thing about this area, is it?"

"Indeed, not!" She repeated. "First there were reports of Master Damon Moreau trying to form a seditious cult to undermine the very structure of Catamondo, then the reports of chupacabra sightings and unexplained deaths began to be reported."

Xander nodded knowingly. "We are here for the same reason." For the first time, since he'd met her, Professor Meowingtons' expression relaxed into something vaguely congenial. "I am sure that when my apprentice saw you, and recalled how knowledgeable you were, she came straight to you, believing you could help us find out what was going on in this area." He gave the professor his most sincere smile. "Can you help us?"

"Possibly." She turned toward the open doorway and called, "Hector, bring me the files on Lucy Fur, Damon Moreau and the purported incidents attributed to the chupacabra."

"Right away, Ma'am!"

Professor Meowingtons turned to Mischief, "You should have told me that you were Master Xander's apprentice instead of merely reminding me who your mother was." Mischief's leaf-green eyes widened and she straightened her little calico spine. "I would gladly help the assistant of such a distinguished Purrtector, whereas I considered the questions of a mere daughter nothing but those of a snoopy kitten."

Mischief tore her attention from the professor and looked at him, uncertainty in her eyes. "I'm your apprentice?"

He tilted both ears forward. "Why do you think I'm pushing you so hard?"

"You're mean."

He laughed. "I can be, but in your case, you need to learn a great deal of information and skills in order to be able to do this job."

"They why haven't you been teaching me to kick-box?"

"There is more than one way to achieve a Purrtectorate posting." He put a question-mark in his tail. "Surely your mother didn't get her posting that way?"

Mischief shook her head. "She is very smart, but not very physical."

"Well there you go, we both are Purrtectors, but arrived at our postings in very different ways. However, no cat has ever become a Purrtector without applying themselves and working hard to learn their lessons."

"What about Merlin? I know you like him a lot and he's the West Coast Purrtector, which is really, really, important, but he's just a pretty-tom!"

Xander laughed so hard his eyes watered. By the time he recovered, a nervous-looking tom, which looked remarkably like the professor, carried an iPhone into the room and placed it in front of the professor.

Professor Meowingtons growled, "Hector, I said files, not phone."

Hector gave her a long-suffering look, then swiped his paw on the screen and tapped a pretty blue icon. A couple more taps and he shoved the phone toward the professor. "The files."

"I prefer paper. You know that."

Hector nodded, as if he'd heard this complaint many times. "Yet they are not as stable as cyber storage." Hector turned to Xander and added, "The big flood of '04 ruined our paper files, but we were able to retrieve most of the files on hard drives, so I try to keep this office as paperless as possible."

"Good to know," Xander said.

Hector tilted his head and scrutinized Xander. "Why are you here?"

"That is on a need to know basis and you don't need to know," Professor Meowingtons said. "In fact, there is no one here with me. No one at all."

Hector signed. "Of course there isn't, mother." Aha, he was right, they were related. "Is there anything else I can help you with?"

"Return to whatever you were working on."

"Hurricane preparations, then." Hector left.

Hurricane? Xander carefully tapped his collar to access the weather program and Mars smacked his paw. "Whats yous trings toss dos? Takes outs mys eyes?" Mars softly hissed in his ear.

"Just want to check the weather."

"Is dos its." There was a small movement at his throat, then the weather recording for his area began playing. "Ohs," Mars hissed, "this is nos goods. Hurricanes in twos days is bads, verys, verys, bads."

"True."

"What is?" Professor Meowingtons and Mischief both asked.

"Just talking to myself," Xander said. Professor Meowingtons raised a shaggy brow, then returned to reading the information. Mischief gave his collar a strong look and snorted before she moved close to the professor and started reading, too. Since he was not particularly eager to get too near the professor, Xander crowded next to Mischief, effectively using her as an obstacle between them. Not that he truly believed the professor would actually launch a physical attack, but it never hurt to be safety conscious. "Hmmm. It would be good to record this," Xander murmured.

Mars made a small movement then said, "Dones."

How and when had the chameleon figured out how his collar worked... and was this good or bad? Xander forced himself to focus on the random bits of information listed on the iPhone and tried to mentally put the ones with dates in chronological order.

"Jimani, again," Mischief said. "How come everything seems to be going on there?"

"Very good question, Miss Mischief," Professor Meowingtons said. "I would like to know the answer to that, too. So, why do you think the events in all three of these files seem to take place in or near that city?"

Mischief swallowed so hard that her bright red collar bobbed up and down. "Because, maybe, Tante Lucy had something to do with that nasty witch doctor, Damon, and those chupacabra killings?" Professor Meowingtons arched both wildly bushy brows. Mischief inhaled, then quickly added, "Or maybe the witch doctor and those nasty chupacabras want something from Tante Lucy?"

"Very good, you're seeing the situation from more than one perspective." Professor Meowingtons practically purred. "What else?"

Mischief gave Xander a quick, desperate look, and he realized that she was trying not to give out any information, which might be classified, regarding their involvement. He gave her an encouraging smile and underscored it with a nod. Mischief sat up taller. "That maybe... probably... Damon and those beasts are working together either with or against Tante Lucy?" Mischief's forehead puckered. "Do you think she's okay? I mean, she hasn't been in the headlines for weeks and weeks, and that's not like her, at all."

"And that's one of the reasons we're going to The Dominican Republic," Xander said. "However, that is classified," he reminded the professor.

"Rest assured, your trip will not be mentioned unless – or until – you expressly give me permission to do so."

"I appreciate that." And he did. "By any chance, do you have a home address for her? My records show her address as being in Santo Domingo, but they also mention that her main home is in Jimani." Xander's tail swished, displaying his frustration over the incomplete files. "I don't even have next of kin or family-line listed."

"That's not unheard of for a stray," Professor Meowingtons said.

"I didn't realize she was," Xander said in surprise. Then he frowned and turned his attention on Mischief, "If she was a stray, why do you refer to her as your aunt?"

"A few years ago, after a big flood – you know, the kind that washed away houses and all sorts of stuff and killed lots and lots of cats and dogs and even people and cows?"

"Yes, I've heard of those," he said.

"Well, mama's house was one of them that got washed away."

"Wait! Your mother was from here?"

Mischief nodded. "When she was a baby. I think she was two weeks old, when that flood happened, and she nearly died, but she didn't and she got taken to a shelter and Tante Lucy was there and just a few months older and it was mostly just them and a lot – I mean a real lot – of dogs, so they decided they would be each other's family and even though they adopted humans in different countries, they still think of each other as family and if Tante Lucy is my mama's family then she's mine, too." She ended her complicated explanation with a decisive nod of her black, gold and white head.

"Works for me," Xander said.

"I didn't realize you're dear mother was from here or that she had been through such an awful flood," Professor Meowingtons said. "I thought she was from Port-au-Prince."

"Well, yeah, she adopted a human from there, so moved when she was about two months old, then she went to the local Academy and has lived there just about all her life."

Professor Meowingtons nodded in understanding, then cautiously tapped the face of the iPhone with her claw. "Let me see if I can find any mention of where Lucy's home in Jimani might be." When the screen when blank, she rolled out a plastic-covered map, which kept trying to roll itself back up, and tapped her claw against it. "We are here and if Miss Fur went to her farm, she is there." She tapped the map, near the shore of Étang Saumâtre. Xander estimated her farm was not far from where he had previously seen her launch the boat for her meeting with Chester. "And, Jimani is here." the professor's paw, again moved slightly East, before her claw tapped the map.

"Where is the border?" Mischief asked.

"Here." The professor indicated a spot, which was nearly on top of the location she had said was Lucy's farm.

"What sort of farm is it?" he asked.

"Egg... Specifically chickens and eggs, but with the current bird-flu crisis, I imagine there could be problems, which is why I was not overly surprised when she returned from the city to purrsonally oversee the farm."

"Good to know," Xander said.

"Is bird flu contagious?" Mischief asked.

"I don't know," the professor said. Judging by her inflection, that admission was quite unpleasant for her to make.

A loud boom shook the building. Mischief jumped straight up, landing in attack pose and looked wildly for an assailant, while the professor spun around, as if expecting an assault from the rear. In the other room, he heard something get dropped and at least one yowl of fright. Were it not for his extensive training, Xander knew he would have done the same thing. When both of them realized it was only thunder, they tried to camouflage their reactions. Always a gentleman, Xander pretended he hadn't noticed anything.

"Xander! Where are you?" Sharkey called. "Are you hurt?"

"In here," he meowed. "And yes, I'm fine. It's just the weather." Before he finished his sentence, Sharkey and Scar appeared in the doorway. He gallantly turned to the professor, whose eyes looked big as pumpkins, as she stared at the black and white pair standing in her doorway. "Professor Meowingtons, allow me to present my associates, Ms. Sharkey and Mr. Scar... Sharkey, Scar, meet Mischief's previous professor, who is also on the board of directors for The Daily Mews. She has been very helpful with information about the area we are headed for."

Sharkey confidently entered the room and gave the professor a respectful cheek rub, but though Scar smiled at her, he moved out of the doorway, kept his back to the wall and appeared to be looking for a place to hide.

"Associates?" Professor Meowingtons managed to say.

Xander inclined his head. "Yes. The Council assigned Ms. Sharkey to assist me as I investigate Ms. Lucy Fur's possible disappearance and Mr. Scar has been very helpful providing information about certain individuals whom might be of interest."

Her wild fur bristled even more. "SO, there is a lot more to this situation."

"Perhaps. Perhaps not. Either way, once I deduce the facts, I shall be happy to share them with you."

"Indeed you will!" Despite more wall-shaking thunder, the professor sat back down at the map and told them all she knew.

Xander hoped it was enough.

Chapter 5

Xander climbed the sturdy trunk of a tree, which he calculated would have a good view of Lucy Fur's poultry farm. He found a position on a branch, where he could study the valley below and focused on the two long structures, which were very similar to the long, low barn, which had been used for drying catnip at the Isla Moreau property. Like the Moreau property, the house was at least a quarter mile from the barns. Was this set-up of the buildings coincidence? If so, why did one long low building have open sides, like the one at Isla Moreau, but only have a big pile of boxes and two tractor-type machines inside, while the other long low barn had walls without windows?

A quick consult with his collar resulted in a hiss from Mars, who was still covering it and the information that the two odd tractors were a loader-backhoe and a forklift.

Why would those be needed on a poultry farm? He consulted his collar and discovered that chickens pooped a whole lot and a forklift could be used to move pallets of eggs or cages of chickens going to slaughter, so those machines would be useful. Even more interesting, commercial egg farm barns usually didn't have windows because the light inside was controlled artificially to increase egg production. While that explained why there could be valid differences between the barns, many questions remained.

Did this farm camouflage another hidden laboratory? Or should he focus on the differences? At Isla Moreau, the house had two stories and a big wrap-around porch. Unless it had a basement, this house only had one floor and a deep porch on one side.

And did that barn have walls without windows because chickens needed artificial light or might it hide something worse?

Furthermore, there was a lot of empty space in the barn without walls, so why was more stuff piled outside, than inside?

"This tree reminds me of Jamaica," Sharkey said.

Xander immediately recalled the flame tree in which she had gotten one of the huge vermilion flowers stuck to her ear by a cobweb. He smiled at her. "These are excellent lookout posts. We can see for miles without being seen."

"Strange that there are so few trees in this country," Sharkey said.

"Mama says that years ago, humans cut down just about all the trees, but she never said why they did such a dumb thing," Mischief said. "And Professor Meowingtons said that deforestation – that's the word for when all the trees are gone – makes all kinds of problems because without the tree leaves to catch it, rain comes down too hard and the ground can't take the abuse, so deforestation is why the flood in this country are so horrible. She says there will be more really, really bad floods, too."

"Indeed," Sharkey said, in a rather good imitation of the professor.

Xander was simply glad that there was a forty-foot high tree where he needed it, and that its branches had enough feathery, fern-like green leaves and huge orange-red flowers to hide them from prying eyes.

"Did you know that the seeds from these are used to make maracas?" Mischief asked.

"No," Xander said, as he tried to understand the pattern of activity at the farm, and not to wonder why anyone would want to make a maraca – whatever that was.

"Whats ares thos piles ofs rocks?" Mars whispurred into his ear.

"Not rocks. The things in the geometrical square stacks are eggs in some sort of holder and the huge piles of lumpy things are bags full of something."

"Thos is tos bigs fors eggs."

"Chicken eggs are a lot bigger than chameleon eggs." He licked his lips, remembering Ginny's scrambled eggs. "But you're right, it's odd for them to just be sitting there in the sun." Particularly when there was plenty of room to protect them in the open-sided barn.

"You're talking to Mars, aren't you?" Mischief asked.

"Yes," he said. "We're trying to figure out why the humans – I mean it must have been humans, because who else would bother to stack eggs in strange lumpy gray containers like that and then pile them all in equal, geometric heaps in the sun?" He stared at the rectangular piles of what must be eggs, which were in front of a small hill of whitish bags. He'd seen that sort of bag before and assumed they contained chicken food.

"Doesn't make sense, does it?" Sharkey asked.

No, it didn't, but then, if humans didn't have proper guidance, they often seemed to do bizarre things, like pile thousands of eggs in the sun or cut down trees for no good reason. What bothered him was that if this actually was Lucy Fur's farm, why was she allowing this sort of thing to happen? Allowing perfectly good food to go bad was not something a good Purrtector would do.

The heavy, throaty sound of a diesel engine drifted up the hill. Xander watched as the mustard-colored loader-backhoe clanked away from the barns, then stopped in the middle of an untended field and began using the long, clumsy-looking backhoe to dig a hole. He tilted his head, as he wondered why the human had chosen that spot to dig.

"Wonder why they're doing that," Mischief said.

"The ground on which we stand is sacred ground. It is the dust and blood of our ancestors. Chief Plenty Coups of the Crow said that."

"Right," Mischief said, "but it still doesn't explain why they're digging a big ole hole there." Suddenly, she crouched low, as if trying to hide and hissed, "Is that D-Damon?"

Xander looked toward the walled barn she was staring at, where a big black cat had just emerged from the door. "Could be, but it is too far away for me to tell what color its eyes are."

"Why is that important?" Sharkey asked. "That's the biggest, shiniest black cat I've ever seen. How could you not be able to recognize him?"

"Since there's only one, it's probably D-Damon," Mischief said.

"Unless either Matsu or Mingus died in the fire, which would mean there was only one," Xander said, then turned to Sharkey, "In answer to your question, all three of them were very large, and were all shiny black. Matsu and Mingus were the same size and seemed to always be together and even walk alike, while Damon was a bit larger."

"And he had purple eyes... really, really eerie purple eyes," Mischief said.

Sharkey snorted, "Cats don't have purple eyes."

"True, but Damon does," Xander said.

"Really, really scary ones," Mischief said. "I'm glad we're watching him from here."

Xander was, too, particularly if the professor's information about there being bird flu on this farm was accurate. That nasty disease was deadly to most birds. Worse, other mammals could catch the virus from sick birds. He scratched his ear, as he recalled that Dr. Moreau had included parrot DNA when she had created Lucy Fur. If the chickens on her farm had contracted the horrible illness, might she be sick, too?

"Is possibles," Mars whispurred, confirming Xander's suspicions that the chameleon was capable of reading his thoughts.

Sharkey quit staring at the loader-backhoe and rubbed her eyes, then looked around and frowned. "Where's Scar?"

Xander looked around, too. "Good question.... Hey, Scar, where are you hiding?" There was no answer. And no matter how patiently he looked for movement in the branches above and below, he didn't see the rat. Where could he have gone?

"Is that him?" Mischief asked, as she pointed to a very small whitish movement heading down the hillside. "And if so, how come he's going to the farm? I thought you said that you wanted us to surveil, er, survey everything, so we knew who was there and what was going on before we went there."

Xander glared at the small whitish movement, which was making a beeline, or rather a rat-line, from his surveillance platform to the farm. He could only think of one reason for such disobedience. "The traitor!"

"He wouldn't tattle on us to those misfits," Mischief said.

"They are his taxa, we're cats and cats are known to eat rats," Xander said.

"Well, yeah, but he didn't choose his family, he chose us for his furiends." Mischief's tail twitched. "Furiends are better than family because we have a choice." She gave a decisive nod.

Sharkey eagerly nodded in agreement. "That is so true."

"Then why is he heading down there instead of helping us survey the situation?" Xander asked.

Mischief's nose reddened so deep that her white nose turned a vague pink. Her defiant posture slumped. "I don't know."

Sharkey, who hadn't taken her gaze off the rat, said, "Gluttony?"

"Huh?" Mischief asked.

"Well, yes, he is heading to the farm, but it looks like he is specifically heading either toward those eggs or whatever is in those bags. My guess is that his stomach is guiding him."

"He does like eating," Mischief said. "Just because someone doesn't do exactly like you tell them, doesn't mean they are a traitor or somethin' and I know that's what you were thinking about him." Mischief narrowed her eyes. "You think you are the boss of everyone, but you're wrong." So, the insubordination was out in the open. Good, now he could deal with it. Mischief's tail quivered with anger. "Before you judge him, watch to see what he does." With a decisive nod she turned her attention to Scar.

Xander perked his ears as he studied her. "Are you angry at me for thinking your furiend could be a traitor or because I want you to succeed and push you in a way, which I know will give you a good future?"

Mischief whirled to face him so fast that she nearly lost her footing on the branch. "You don't care about my future! You're just jealous because I can swim and am learning to ride a boogie board and you don't want me showing you up!" Sharkey started laughing so hard that her eyes watered. "What's so funny?"

"You!" Sharkey laughed harder.

Mischief looked angry enough to burst.

"What makes you think that I would be dumb enough to move aboard a boat and not know how to swim?" Xander asked.

"Well, you never have."

"I haven't needed to."

"Most ca-cats do-don't like wa-water," Sharkey said, "That do-doesn't me-mean we can't swim."

Mischief's eyes widened. "You can swim?" Sharkey nodded. "And you? You can swim?" Much as he hated to admit it, Xander nodded, too. "I don't believe it!" Mischief's ears flattened. "You're just saying that to make me think my talent isn't special."

"Your obsession with water is certainly unusual," Xander said.

Mischief glared at him. "You're just jealous of my talent." Sharkey laughed so hard she fell off the branch and barely caught herself on a lower one. "What's wrong with her?"

"She obviously has heard about Cha-Cha's rescue, which helped me become a Purrtector. It was in the Puget Sound and required water skills." Xander shrugged. "Before that, I was just a jock who won a lot of kick-boxing tournaments. But that is ancient history. My point is that I'm the adult and you're the kitten. I've had a lot of time to learn several things, but the most important thing I've learned is that Academy lessons are very important because, if you learn what mistakes were made in the past, you can avoid them in the future."

Mischief shook her head. "You just think you know, but you don't."

Xander studied her and wondered how he could talk sense to the thick-headed little calico.

"Yep," Sharkey said, "The rat was after food."

Xander glanced down at her, then at the stacks of eggs, where Scar was indeed gorging. His nose wrinkled in distaste.

"What, now?" Mischief said. "Don't even tell me you don't like eggs, 'cause I've seen you eat hundreds of them."

"True, but not eggs that may or may not have been laid by sick birds or ones that have been stacked in the sunlight, for Hathor-knows-how-long to go bad."

For the first time, Mischief looked uncertain. "You think he could get sick from eating them?"

"It's possible." He raised a brow. "Don't you think it's odd for all those eggs to be stacked that far away from the buildings, where they must have been laid?" He pointed to an open-sided shed, which was half-empty. "There was plenty of space to protect them from the weather there, and that even is right next to the road, so why are those stacks so far away from the buildings and a convenient way to ship them?"

Mischief's forehead wrinkled in thought, then she opened her mouth to say something, but quickly shut it.

Perhaps the kitten was learning.

Xander watched Scar for a moment, then studied the area as a whole. "Does anyone else think it's odd that the only activity we see is a loader-backhoe digging a huge hole in pasture?"

"I've been wondering about that," Sharkey said.

Mischief kept her mouth shut.

Yep, the kitten was learning that one didn't acquire knowledge and understanding by talking; they got it by watching, feeling, sniffing, listening and thinking.

A big shadow passed over the ground, near the flame tree they were in, and cruised downhill toward the sprawling farm.

"What was that?" Mischief meowed.

"Probably a vulture," Sharkey whispurred.

As second shadow passed, Xander recognized the silhouette. "It's Clade and Allele."

Mischief gasped.

Sharkey look mystified. "It's what and what?"

"The Vi-Purrs," Mischief said. "They're two really, really scary taxa." She looked up at Xander, her eyes big, frightened jade pools. "You don't think they'll hurt poor Scar, do you?"

Xander, who didn't know what to expect from something as awful as Clade and Allele, simply shrugged. "Let's watch and see."

The Vi-Purrs continued gliding toward the farm house, As they approached the outer buildings, they were barely over the roofs. If they glanced to their right, they would surely see the rat gorging itself on eggs, or at least wonder about all the broken shells and mess littering the ground by the stack that Scar seemed to be trying to eat.

Was it his imagination or was the rat visibly fatter? One of the Vi-Purrs screeched. Involuntarily, the seal point fur on Xander's spine stood at attention, but he quickly calmed his nerves.

Still, Claude and Allele flew toward the house, and landed near the steps to the deep porch. A red cat greeted them, but at this distance, even with his acute vision, Xander couldn't tell if it was Chester or Lucy Fur. While it was logical to assume that if this was Ms. Lucy's farm, she would be the one to greet visitors, it was equally logical that if Clade and Allele were here, they were helping Chester with some plot to dominate Catamondo, or whatever else they figured they could overpower.

If Lucy Fur had died of the bird flu, it would explain why the farm appeared to be running in such a disorganized manner, with valuable eggs sitting in the sun, instead of in a protected place, where they could easily be loaded onto a truck. It could also explain why her staff was digging a huge hole in the middle of a pasture, for no apparent reason. And it would certainly explain why she hadn't been in the catarazzi spotlight for weeks.

He narrowed his eyes at the red cat, but since Chester and Lucy Fur were the same color, it was impossible to tell which one of them was apparently lecturing Clade and Allele, who seemed to be agitated about something.

Had they spotted Scar as they flew in?

If so, why hadn't they landed near him? Did they need some sort of permission from their leader?

The door opened and a gigantic black cat came out. It was easily three times the size of Chester. Matsu and Mingus had been noticeably larger than Chester, but Xander was fairly sure this giant was Damon.

"Merlin's hunch was right," Xander whispurred.

"Seems sos," Mars whispurred back. "Yous wants mes tos gets closes ands makes sures?"

"It would be dangerous."

"Mores dangerous nots tos knows."

The chameleon had a valid point. "But that's a long way for someone with such short legs to go."

"Is figures yous takes mes tos thes barns."

"You did? How come?"

"What are you whispurring about?" Sharkey asked.

"Discussing a plan with Mars."

"Afternoons storms bes heres soons. Trees nots safes places ins storms."

Xander twisted around to look to the East; the horizon was dark. How could he have been so focused on the farm not to notice the danger coming behind him? "We need to head for that open-sided barn." He moved back to the trunk and began climbing down.

"How come it's safe for us to go now?" Mischief asked.

"It isn't safe, but it's safer than getting caught in the highest tree around with a storm coming."

With yelps of surprise, Mischief and Sharkey scurried toward the trunk. Soon, the three of them were high-tailing it down the slope toward the promising shelter of the open-sided barn. They got there moments before the water began drumming against the metal roof in such a heavy, noisy deluge, that it looked like a solid wall of water surrounded the building. Even if they had been spotted, it was doubtful if anyone or anything would venture out until the rain quit.

Thunder boomed directly overhead and lightening hit the ground so close that his fur stood on end.

"I am so glad we left the tree when we did!" Sharkey said.

"Me, too," Mischief said, in a voice so faint that she could barely be heard over the drumming on the metal roof.

Thunder boomed, right over them, again.

Mars shivered, which reminded Xander that his collar's sensors were on – a situation that wasn't good with lightning so close, particularly when under a metal roof. No sooner did he have the thought, than he felt Mars move to turn his collar off. This alliance was as handy as it was disconcerting.

"Is that thing coming our direction?" Sharkey asked. Her attention was on the far end of the building where a roundish, yellowish light seemed to be getting bigger.

He heard the guttural growl of a diesel engine beneath the din from the rain pounding against the roof. "Backhoe! Hide!" A quick glance confirmed that the only possible shelter was either in the exposed rafters, under the forklift or in the deep shadows under the three pallets stacked with boxes. "Under the pallets! Quick!"

Without asking why he'd chosen them, both Sharkey and Mischief dashed there and easily slid under. It was a more difficult squeeze for him. The rough concrete floor was cool and the shadows quickly hid them from the machine, which was getting steadily closer.

"It smells wonderful here." Mischief said.

"It sure does," Sharkey agreed. "I wonder why I smell the best catnip ever, when this is a chicken and egg farm."

"Don't know," Mischief said, "but at the other farm they used a barn this size to dry herbs."

"Then they're obviously connected, but I still don't understand the catnip connection."

"My mama thought that Damon was trying to get cats addicted so that he could man-ip-u-late them."

"Interesting, but why would he want to do that?"

"She figured it was a power thing."

"Shh," Xander said, as the loader's front bucket moved through the curtain of water.

"You think the driver can hear us over the noise from rain and the engine?" Mischief asked.

"No, but I also think the weather is unpredictable and the driver will turn off the engine, so it could get quiet quick and we do not want to be talking when that happens."

Mischief nodded.

"Grown men can learn from very little children for the hearts of the little children are pure. Therefore, the Great Spirit may show to them many things which older people miss. Black Elk of the Oglala Lakota Sioux said that." Mischief gave Sharkey a pleased smile and Xander wondered if she thought Sharkey had given her a compliment, but, as usual, Sharkey's quotations didn't make any sense to him. If Mischief got something out of them, perhaps it was a girl-thing.

The backhoe came to a stop in the center of the building and the driver tilted the big front bucket, causing gallons of water to dump on the floor and stream toward him. He should have chosen the rafters. High ground was always better, but he doubted that Mischief could have gotten up there and he didn't trust her on her own. Within moments, the first wave of water began to ooze under him.

Mischief gasped. "That's cold!"

Both he and Sharkey said, "Shhh" and not a moment too soon, as the engine shut off. For a second, it seemed quiet, then thunder boomed, farther away this time, but still too close for comfort, plus the rain was still drumming against the metal roof as if Hathor had opened the flood gates of the Ever-after.

Skinny brown feet landed on the floor. Xander peered at the driver, wondering if the thin, latino-looking human with the long, thick coils of rain-soaked black hair was another one of Dr. Moreau's creations or if he was actually a full-human. The man's denim cut-offs and tan T-shirt clung to his lean frame and he looked mostly human, wet, but human. Of course, that didn't mean a lot since Rufus looked more-or-less human, too. But while Rufus was hairy, this person was bare, except for the long, straggly coils of hair on his head, which sort of looked like black snakes, which were dripping water into a puddle around him as he stared out at the weather.

Since the person was only paying attention to the rain and wringing water from his hair and shirt, Xander felt confident studying him. Or was it a her? Men normally didn't have hair halfway down their backs, did they? Deciding that gender was irrelevant, Xander continued looking for clues about the person's origins and concluded that if he or she could wring his or her hair out like that, it was very doubtful that the person's head-covering was any sort of feathers or Medusa-like snakes. Still, the hair appeared to be about the same color as Damon, Mingus and Matsu, so he couldn't rule out the possibility that the person was some sort of taxa.

Mischief crept close enough to whispurr in his ear, "If this building had a basement, like that other barn, don't you think she would have gone down?"

"She?"

Mischief gestured to the dripping human. Could his apprentice be correct about the gender? Did it matter? Wasn't the important part of her question the suggestion that if this building had a basement, the human would have gone to the hidden access to escape the storm?

Why hadn't he thought of looking for a secret space, here?

By the time the drumming on the metal roof was calmer, his tummy and paws were soaked with muddy water and the stench of diesel fumes mixed with the pleasant scent of herb, giving him a headache.

"I feel a little sick," Mischief said.

"It's the diesel," he whispurred back. "Lie down on that dry, wood slat, close your eyes and try to relax. As soon as the breeze clears the air, you'll feel better."

"You sure?"

Since Whispurring Winds had a diesel engine, which theyused on occasion, but had not needed since Mischief had joined him, he was able to give her a confident nod, which knocked the back of his head against the pallet above.

Mars grunted.

Despite the wet floor, and having an interesting person to watch, Xander settled flat as possible on the wet concrete, next to the wooden upright portion, closed his eyes and tried to relax, too. Mischief snuggled close and the muscles in her little body loosened.

The next thing he knew, a ripping sound woke him. He jerked upright and hit the top of his head for the second time. Mischief jumped, too, and upon landing, she dashed out from under the pallet of boxes. Xander shook his head to clear the stars and tried to remain clear-headed. The rain had stopped and the air was heavy with the enticing scent of catnip. Odd that he thought the word 'enticing' as it concerned 'nip. He had never understood the obsession so many cats displayed for the herb or why they claimed it smelled divine – until now. He must have hit his head harder than he thought.

Xander crawled out from under the pallet in time to see Mischief climbing the boxes. The man was gone and it was dark, so perhaps some of the stars he saw were actually in the sky. Xander closed his eyes and most of the stars vanished. He sighed in relief, then opened his eyes and jumped to the top of the stack of boxes, landing next to Sharkey, who had apparently ripped one box open. The amazing scent was coming from inside. A glance showed dozens of fancy cat toys, which were decorated with feathers and each enclosed in its own transparent plastic bag. His ears flattened, as he tried to understand why Sharkey had opened the box. When he couldn't think of a good reason, he asked.

"I wanted to see what they were sending to so many Purrtectorates."

"Those are so cool!" Mischief said, "You don't think they'd miss one, do you? I mean the box is open and all." She stared longingly at the plastic-wrapped bags. "Those toys are so cute! I don't need to wait to get mine, do I?" Xander slammed the lid shut and sat on it, lest he, too be tempted. Mischief glared at him. "You're such a meanie."

"Why not let the kid have a toy?" Sharkey said.

Xander glared at her. "Think about where you are."

"Sitting on top of a box of super cute toys and not being allowed to play with one," Mischief said.

"On a chicken and egg farm, which your beloved Professor Meowingtons said had bird flu," Xander said. "Think about what we've seen since we got here: hundreds of eggs sitting in the sun going bad; a backhoe digging a pit and my guess is that they intend to bury something in it; perhaps the eggs, or maybe dead birds, too. - I haven't seen or heard any birds, except those Vi-Purrs, have you?" Mischief shook her head. "And now boxes of toys." He turned his attention on Sharkey. "How do you know these are being sent to Purrtectorates?"

She tilted an ear toward a clipboard, which had a long typed list and big red checkmarks on each line. "There are a thousand toys in each box. I really don't think one or two would be missed."

Both of Xander's ears flattened. "Were those toys so cute that you'd be willing to die in exchange for a bit of fun playing with one?"

Sharkey's golden eyes widened. "What do you mean?"

"He means that those toys are meant to make us sick," Mischief said. "Are you sure that cats can get a bird disease?"

"Do you want to gamble that you can't?" She shook her head. "What I am sure of is that Chester, Damon or whoever is sending out these boxes wants to undermine Catamondo any way they can and I wager that they have the scientific ability to mutate a virus to cross species."

Mischief's nose turned white. "I don't want one anymore." She looked around frantically. "We need to destroy them before they leave here and infect everyone."

"That would be ideal, but purrhaps not the best choice," Xander said.

"Why not?" Sharkey asked.

"If we destroy them here, they know we're on to them and they'll disappear and come up with another plan from somewhere we don't know about."

Mischief nodded. "That's what they did, last time. First they wanted to make a phony Purrsident Mitzi they could use to get control of our government, now toys." She shivered. "I'd hate to think what they came up with next, but how can we be sure that these don't get out and make kittens sick?"

"I haven't got that worked out, yet, but I'll start with sending out a warning to all Purrtectors, so if any boxes manage to get delivered, they'll be destroyed before getting opened and releasing the virus."

"What if Chester has hacked our messaging service?" Sharkey said, "Or what if one or more of the other Purrtectors are his taxa? If you send a message to everyone, that could be just as much of a red flag to that bunch as destroying these toys here and now."

She had a valid point. "We know we can trust Sir Simon," he looked at Mischief, "and your mom."

"You always include Ms. Fluffy and Mr. Merlin," Mischief said.

"So, out of thousands of Purrtectors, we only trust four?" Sharkey bit her lower lip. "I can't believe they would make something that smelled so good and looked like so much fun into a bad thing."

"That's 'cause you don't know how warped that bunch is," Mischief said. Her little forehead furrowed, "How come they don't get sick? I mean, they're part bird, aren't they? Wouldn't they be more likely to get sick from this than just a regular cat?"

Xander nodded. "Did you notice anything special about the toys?"

"What-cha mean?" Mischief asked.

Sharkey's eyes widened so much that white showed all around. "Red feathers... there were one of two tiny red feathers among the white, beige and brown ones on each of the toys that I saw." She swallowed. "Do you think it's like that for all of them?"

"That would be my guess." Xander said.

Mischief looked mystified for a moment, then she, too, figured out what he and Sharkey suspected. "Oh, they're even worse than I imagined. You think that Tante Lucy got sick with that flu and maybe even died, like the chickens, and they plan to use her fur with those sick feathers to make other cats sick?" She began to sob.

Xander nodded. The only question was if Lucy Fur had survived the illness or if she had been plucked after she passed. Either way, it explained why her efforts hadn't been in the news recently. "I'm fairly sure the Dominican Republic will need a new Purrtector, but I don't dare report this to the Council, yet."

Mischief wiped away her tears, but looked shaken. "Purrhaps Professor Meowingtons could do something."

"Like what?" Sharkey asked.

"I don't know for sure, but she knows everyone and has lived here for ages. Surely she would know how a new Purrtector could get appointed or voted in or whatever happens in a case like this."

The kitten just might have a valid point. If the Professor instituted a coup, it might work to distract the Moreau cats from what was really going on. "We'll think about this, but for now, I need to get a copy of that list and you," he looked at Sharkey, "need to retape that box... As for you," he told teary-eyed Mischief, "you need to get up into the rafters."

"Why?"

"Because you can be the lookout, plus we can't stay under the pallet. Now that the weather is clearing, they're probably going to ship them. Do you want to be under there when the forklift rams its forks under?" She shook her head. "I didn't think so. So go on."

"I can't jump that high or climb those slick posts."

Xander looked from her to the beam, which was only four or five feet above the stacked boxes, then, before he could think better of it, grabbed her by the scruff of her calico neck, leaped up and deposited her on the beam. He was already hopping back down when she squeaked in outrage, "Stop treating me like a baby!"

Ignoring her, Xander proceeded to tap his collar so he could record the information on the clipboard. It took him a second to realize that Mars was no longer camouflaging his collar. Where in the world had the chameleon gone? Had he gotten hurt when he hit his head? As soon as he finished copying all the pages, he hopped to the floor and

checked under the pallets, but there was no sign of Mars there, either.
Sharkey looked down at him. "Lose something?"

"Do you know where Mars is?"

After an intense look at his neck, she shook her head. "Does he often leave without saying anything?"

"It's not the first time." Xander hoped the little guy had gone because of some agenda of his own, like catching bugs for a snack or something, and not because he had gotten hurt by his own clumsiness.

"Well, I'm sure he'll be back," Sharkey said.

"A light just turned on in the house," Mischief said.

"Good job," Xander said, as he hopped back on top of the boxes and from there up onto the beam. "Sharkey, are you about done with that taping job?"

She nodded, then jumped onto a nearby beam. "Between individuals, as between nations, peace means respect for the rights of others. Benito Juarez of the Zapotec said that and I'm pretty sure all three of us on one beam would be too crowded, so I am respecting your rights." With that, Sharkey sprawled on the beam and put her chin on her paws, as she studied the house.

"Don't you ever grab me like that, again," Mischief hissed.

"I'm so glad you appreciate my help," Xander said, as he, too settled down to watch the house and grounds.

He didn't know what woke him, but the sky was lightening at the horizon, which meant it would soon be sunrise. Strange that there was a poultry barn within twenty feet of this open-sided one and he didn't hear any roosters crowing. Was that because the light wasn't visible inside the windowless barn, or perhaps they only had hens? He frowned so hard that his whiskers drooped, as he realized that the only evidence he had seen of any chickens being in the vicinity was a few thousand eggs and the feathers decorating the dangerous toys. He hadn't seen any actual birds, not even the ones the feathers had come from.

Why not?

Where were the birds?

The house's door opened and the skinny human with the long coils of hair came out. He or she put on a jacket, while briskly walking toward his location. Xander glanced at Sharkey and Mischief, but both were already as flat and motionless as possible. Excellent that he didn't need to tell them what to do. Xander closed his eyes to slits so that no light could reflect off them and give away his location.

The human went directly to the loader-backhoe and started its engine. As diesel fumes billowed over their location, Mischief gave two very loud, noisy sneezes. Xander tried not to breathe and even felt his own eyes start to tear, so he didn't blame her for her involuntary reaction. "Turn your nose the other direction," he whispurred.

Moving slowly, but steadily, she followed his advice without question.

No sooner had the noisy, smelly machine moved out of the building, than there was movement in the porch's shadows. Xander blinked away the tears so he could see better, then as the first rays of light broke over the hills and bathed the porch in cool light, two familiar forms moved to the edge and flapped their wings to warm their muscles. Then, Clade and Allele let out ear-splitting shrieks and launched themselves into the air. Had they been awake when Sharkey opened the boxes or seen them examining the shipment? Xander swallowed and waited to see what the Vi-Purrs intended to do.

Overhead, there were several more cries as they circled the sky. Were they riding a wave of air or watching the ground to see if he would move?

The loader-backhoe filled its big front bucket with lumpy whitish bags, then headed in the direction of the big hole it had dug. As it moved past, his sensitive nose caught the stench of rotting meat.

Were those bags full of dead chickens?

It certainly smelled like they were. A chill rushed from his nose to the tip of his tail.

Was the bird flu problem that bad or had the poor birds been killed as a precaution?

Hunkered down on the beam, and trying to keep track of Clade and Allele as well as see exactly what the human was doing, Xander had more questions than answers. So, he did the one productive thing that he could do in his circumstances: he activated his collar's correspondence function and sent the information he had acquired to

Merlin and Fluffy, then, he sent individual notes to Purrsey and Professor Meowingtons.

Chapter 6

Later that morning, Xander's empty stomach began to grumble. They needed to do something to keep up their strength.

But what?

Until he had a safe answer for that, it was wisest to stay on the beam and watch the loader-backhoe shuttle lumpy white bags that stank of rotting meat to the swimming pool size hole in the field. Now, that the sun was up, the loader-backhoe's driver had taken off his jacket and had tied a rag over his face, so he looked like an over-large child playing cops and robbers.

"Do you think there are any kerchiefs around here that we could use?" Mischief whispurred.

"For what?" Xander asked.

She gave the passing machine's driver a significant look. "I don't see the human gagging over the stench from the rot or the diesel fumes."

"Do you really think a thin piece of fabric can keep out smells?" Xander cocked an eyebrow. She nodded. "Interesting. What about if I tell you that our sense of smell is about fourteen times as strong as a human's?"

"Did you just make that up?"

He shook his head, and managed not to point out that if she had paid close attention to her lessons, she would have learned that fact a month ago.

Mischief looked around to make sure no one but the machine and its driver were nearby, then waved at Sharkey. "Can humans smell well?" Sharkey's ears perked with surprise and she opened her mouth to answer, then seemed to have second thoughts, so merely shook her head, no.

Xander moved close enough to whispurr in her ear. "It is common knowledge and not something worth jeopardizing this mission over."

Her mouth turned down and her tail twitched with frustration, but, for a change, she didn't argue. Instead, she flattened herself on the beam and hissed, "Get down, something is coming."

He didn't need to be told twice.

A flatbed truck approached the barn from one direction, the loader-backhoe came from another, but worse, Chester and Damon approached from the house.

Dear Hathor, this was not good!

In fact, the only good thing was that Damon was close enough for him to see his vivid purple eyes and the sun glinting off the devil's symbol he proudly wore on his collar. What surprised him was the differential way he tilted his head toward Chester. Did he respect the bright red cat as much as his body language suggested?

The worker parked the loader-backhoe to one side, cut off the engine, and hopped down. Then slipped the rag down, so it hung around his neck. As he approached Chester and Damon, the human bowed low. Chester slightly inclined his head, but Damon merely looked arrogant. Still, Chester was the one who stepped forward to speak to the person, but Xander couldn't hear what was said over the noise of the flatbed truck backing into the barn. The human nodded, then went to the forklift and started it, which added more noise and fuel stench to his already over-taxed ears and nose.

Oh, how he missed his peaceful Whispurring Winds!

Mischief put her paws over her ears as she turned her face away from the two loud engines. If he hadn't needed to see what was happening, he would have done the same thing. Instead, he clicked on his collar's recording program and keyed it to automatically store the data in the clouds, where Merlin and Fluffy would also have access to it.

A glance at Sharkey assured him that she was as flat and still as if she was part of the beam. The girl had done well in training. Now, if they could all avoid sneezing or having their stomachs growl, they might get information instead of get caught.

The tines of the forklift rammed under the first pallet of boxes and within a minute, it was loaded on top of the flatbed truck. In quick succession, the other two pallets were also loaded, then the coil-haired person and the bow-legged truck driver worked together to put a stiff, bright blue piece of fabric over the boxes and rope everything down securely.

No one looked at how the boxes were taped or seemed to notice that one had been opened. Xander didn't have time to savor that stroke of luck because once the truck was loaded, Chester and Damon hopped into the cab. Did they plan to accompany all the boxes to wherever they would be shipped from? It looked like it and this was not good. He quickly keyed in a note to Purrsey and Professor Meowingtons, notifying them of this unexpected and unwanted change of plan. In a moment's inspiration, he added the truck's license plate number, the name of the shipping company that was painted on the truck's door and a brief description of the actual vehicle.

The truck headed out and the coiled-haired human hopped back on the forklift, then, to Xander's surprise, instead of parking the machine, the person drove it out the side of the building, heading toward the stacks of boxed eggs. As the machine's tines disappeared under the eggs, Xander realized that the unmown grass hid the fact that the eggs were stacked on top of more pallets and there were even more eggs than he had initially calculated.

Mischief sneezed.

Turning his attention back to her watery eyes, he noticed that the diesel fumes seemed to have formed a cloud of misery over the beams. With no wind, the fumes could stay there indefinitely and that was not good. It was time to move. With the Vi-Purrs, Damon and Chester gone and the human moving eggs, this was probably the best opportunity they would have to check out the house.

He motioned for Sharkey that they needed to go to the house, then grabbed Mischief by the scruff and jumped down, landing on his hind paws a moment before he settled onto all four. He gently set her on the concrete floor. Sputtering with fury, Mischief surged to her paws. "I told you never, ever to do that to me, again!"

"You would have preferred to stay up there breathing fumes?"

Her watery glare moved from him to the beam and back, but she was still angry.

"Could you have made the jump, with the pallets gone?"

Uncertainty formed in her expressive eyes, but she was saved from any admission of gratitude by Sharkey asking, "Do you think they'll be back soon?"

"There's no way to know, but this is the best chance we've had to see what's in the house."

"What if Mingus and Matsu are in there?" Mischief asked.

"I'm pretty sure they died in the fire."

"How can you be sure?" Sharkey asked.

"I'm not, but in the past day, we've only seen one black cat, Chester, Clade and Allele."

"And that human," Mischief added.

Xander nodded. "The original body count that the team made makes it likely that Mingus and Matsu died in the fire along with Dr. Moreau and the coven or whatever that group would be called."

"Gang," Mischief said.

"Whatever." Xander sighed and started moving toward the house while the human's back was to them. "The point is that unless Clade and Allele are flying overhead, this is our best chance to check out the house, but just in case there are traps, do not touch anything." He hopped onto the porch and headed toward the pet door. A nudge confirmed that it was locked.

"So much for that idea," Sharkey said.

"You give up too easy," Mischief said.

Xander keyed his collar to transmit the door lock code used at Isla Moreau and the door opened. Sharkey gasped. "How did you do that?"

"Their equipment is low tech and transmitted the same code for all the doors at Isla Moreau, so it was worth seeing if it worked on this one, too." He cautiously moved into the house's shadowed interior. "Come in, but stay near the door while I make sure it's safe."

He heard the soft sounds of Mischief and Sharkey enter and the door latch shut. "So you were right," Mischief said.

"About what?" he asked.

"About Tante Lucy being part of the Moreau take over plot."

"Why do you say that?" Sharkey asked.

"The locking code," Mischief said. "If she had really split from her taxa, and didn't want anything to do with them, she would have used a different code to lock her door."

"Good reasoning," Xander said, though he was surprised that she hadn't noticed the similarities in construction of the barns or the fact that four of the taxa acted like they owned this chicken farm. "Now wait here, while I check to make sure there aren't any traps."

He keyed his collar to help detect hidden ambushes and cautiously moved forward. The kitchen was painted such a bright yellow that he imagined it would look sunny, even with the lights off on a moonless night. Finding no problems there, he moved on to what appeared to be a home office. If any written clues were to be found, they should be here. The laptop had a password, but it only took seconds for his collar to break it. He was just starting to review the recent history when he heard a bang in the kitchen and Mischief howl with – glee?

He leaped from the desk and rushed to the kitchen, where Mischief and Sharkey were both standing stock-still in front of a now-open lower cupboard. Unsure why they were so still, he slowed down and approached from an angle.

"Have you ever seen anything so amazing," Mischief whispurred.

Sharkey shook her head, her attention riveted on whatever was inside the cupboard.

What had he overlooked?

What could hold such hypnotic charm? His collar was no help, and merely indicated that canned goods filled the space, but their reaction was not typical for something like that. A snake, perhaps, but not a can.

"Do you think they'd miss one or two?" Sharkey asked.

"No," Mischief said, "but how do you choose?"

Sharkey's tail slashed with frustration. "I don't know, it all looks so good."

Xander moved to where he could see inside the cupboard, which indeed was full of canned goods, specifically hundreds of cans of Elegant Eats with over a dozen cans of every imaginable flavor: Savory Salmon, Chicken Cordon Bleu, Vegan Bon Vivant, Peking Duck, Gourmet Gumbo, and his purrsonal favorite, Decadent Delicacy. His mouth watered as he reached past them to grab a can.

No sooner had he popped the top of his, than Mischief and Sharkey each grabbed a can and copied what he'd done. Unfortunately, Mischief's claws were not strong enough to pop the top on her Savory Salmon, so he reached over and lent her a paw. And for a change, she didn't complain about his help – possibly because she was too busy eating to talk.

Had anything ever tasted so good?

Had he ever been so hungry?

Did the Decadent Delicacy taste so good because he was starving or had someone doctored the food? Taking a protective step back, he had his collar analyze the ingredients, but nothing unusual was noted. Still, this group had a history of using drugs, so Xander remained cautious.

"What's wrong?" Sharkey asked.

"Does this food taste better than usual?"

She blinked in confusion. "I've never tried this brand before, so how could I know?"

"I haven't either," Mischief said, her mouth full, "so don't let him act like he knows how it should taste."

"For your information, I've eaten this a lot, it's only since I left the United States, that I haven't indulged."

Mischief snorted.

Sharkey looked at him over the top of Mischief's head. "Does it taste the same as you remember?"

"Yes and no. It tastes like the best thing ever." She tilted her head, urging him to go on. "After discovering the plot with the catnip toys that smelled better than any catnip ever, I can't help wondering why this food suddenly tastes so good, too."

Sharkey nodded in understanding. "I understand, but don't you think it's because we haven't eaten in over a day and we're starving? In my experience, the hungrier I am, the better anything tastes."

Mischief polished off her can and finally stood up. "Did you really get to eat this gourmet food all the time before?"

"Yep. Merlin used to have cases sent, but that has been impossible since I traded my land address for an anchor."

She snorted. "Why would your friend send you cases?"

Xander frowned as he studied her belligerent posture. "Because he had more of it than he could eat and knew I liked it."

Mischief rolled her eyes to the ceiling. "Oh, I'm sure he had more than he could eat, and he chose to send the overflow all the way across country to you."

Sharkey looked from Mischief to him, then apparently deciding not to get in the middle of the nonsense, went back to eating.

"Didn't he know anyone he liked nearby?" Mischief asked.

"Of course. It's not as if I was the only one that benefited from him having an unlimited supply."

"Oh, it's an unlimited supply, now. You never mentioned that your friend Merlin was so wealthy."

"He isn't." Xander tapped the picture on the handsome white cat on the Elegant Eats label. "He's the spokes-cat."

She snorted. "Right." Her tail twitched with anger. "Don't you think that I know your friend Merlin is the West Coast Purrtector?"

"Yes, he's that, too." Xander resumed eating.

"You're serious?" He glanced up at his insubordinate apprentice, gave a short nod, then continued eating. As he and Sharkey were finishing, thunder boomed.

"Does this area get storms every afternoon?" Sharkey asked.

"I think it's 'cause of the tropical storm in the Bahamas," Mischief said. "Mama says weather is always worse when one of those is in the area, and the only thing worse is a hurricane."

"That storm was upgraded to a hurricane yesterday," Xander said.

"How -" Mischief looked at his collar. "-never mind."

"Do we need to worry about it?" Sharkey asked.

"I'd worry more if we were on the North side of the island or down in a valley that could be flooded, but we should be fine here." He paused to listen to the sound of the forklift coming closer. "However, the human will probably soon be coming here to stay dry, so we need to put our cans and lids in the trash and go somewhere he won't notice us."

"You mean we should stay in here?" Mischief squeaked. "What if those Vi-purrs come back or Damon or Chester? We can't stay here!"

"Would you prefer to be out in the storm or inside with a good supply of food?"

She put her can in the trash. "The last one, of course, but not when the house belonged to something like Damon and I didn't know when he'd come back."

"The kid has a point," Sharkey said. "Between individuals, as between nations, peace means respect for the rights of others. Benito Juarez of the Zapotec said that."

"Quite right," Xander said, "But I am not about to go out in a thunderstorm much less a potential hurricane, when our safest bet is staying here. Just not here in the kitchen." He and Sharkey both put their cans in the trash, then he led the way back to the home office. "See anything interesting here?"

"The window seat," Mischief said.

"The bookcase," Sharkey said.

Xander nodded as he shut the lid of the laptop. "Exactly, the construction of the window seat and the bookcase doesn't line up, so I'm fairly sure the bottom of that window seat is some sort of hidden compartment." He quickly moved across the room and gave it a closer inspection.

"If the pet door here and the doors at Isla Moreau were all the same whatever-you-call-it," Mischief said.

"Frequency," he said.

"Right, frequency. Then, if there is a hidden door here, wouldn't it probably be that frequency, too?"

"Good thinking." No sooner did his collar emit it than the hidden door slid sideways. He would have preferred to make a cautious inspection of the space, but he heard heavy footsteps on the porch, so instead, he went in and told them, "Follow me." By the time the front door squeaked open, the hidden door was closed and they were huddled in the dark. He took a calming breath and recalled how the lights had been set up to automatically turn on at Isla Moreau. So many things were similar between this chicken farm and the other one that he stepped toward the darkest point with confidence, but by his third step, he began to doubt that this theory would pan out, so he felt ahead with his left paw, and only felt space where the floor should have been. Fortunately, his eyes had begun adapting to the dark and he could vaguely see steep steps leading downward. Again, he reached forward, but this time, down as well. The step was as narrow and steep as a ladder, but seemed solid enough to go a step or two more. By the second step, blinding lights came on. Behind him, Mischief and Sharkey gasped in surprise.

Xander paused, eyes closed, as he listened for tell-tale sounds and sniffed the air.

He smelled Mars. Why in the world would he smell him here? Or was Mars' subtle scent typical of his species? He opened his eyes and wasn't surprised to discover that he was in fact on a ladder, which led to a hidden basement, which was very similar to the one at Isla Moreau and Mars was standing on the middle of the paper-strewn table looking at him, surprise in his big, round, brown eyes. "I wondered where you went," Xander said.

"Iss tols yous, Iss gets closes ands makes sures alls is goods."

"That you did," Xander said as he proceeded down the ladder. "Guess I just didn't expect you to leave during a storm." Outside thunder boomed making him jump over the final four steps.

"Storms almosts overs ands nose humans goes tos houses." Mars puffed out his neck. "Iss takes opportunities."

"Good for you. What have you discovered?"

For several minutes, Xander learned that Mars had not been able to leave the basement area after he'd moved from the human's clothing to Chester's collar, which Mars snorted over and claimed to be deficient of technology. Xander listened to the chameleon's report and made sure that he didn't point out that deficient as Chester's collar was, without it, he would have effectively been trapped. He also learned that Damon was too big to fit through the hidden door, Chester talked to himself and that Mingus and Matsu had passed over in the fire, which Chester thought proved how superior he was.

Mischief snorted at that one, but Xander motioned for her to listen.

After giving Mischief a disgruntled look, Mars indeed continued to tell him about Chester's plan to bring down Catamondo by "killing off the inferior cats with their addictions and proclivity to play with ridiculous toys"

"Do you know why he wants to do that?" Sharkey asked

Good question and one he suspected he had the answer to, but confirmation would be nice.

Mars proceeded to tell them how Chester had ranted about Catamondo refusing to acknowledge and register him. That since they refused to accept him – a fact that he believed was due to his purrsonal superiority – he concluded that Catamondo was too inferior to appreciate him and needed to be destroyed, so he could create a new, improved society. Better yet, he could create a new, improved species of cat.

And, of course, Chester Moreau would control them all, just as he controlled all the other taxa. After that statement, Mars got a strange expression on his tiny face. "What?" Xander asked.

But the chameleon didn't respond.

"He's wondering the same thing we all are," Sharkey said. "He's wondering if Chester somehow controls Rufus and Scar and that's why he somehow manages to stay ahead of us and get away, even when our investigators were certain he and the rest died in the fire."

Mars nodded.

"And Mr. Mars is also probably wondering how many Purrtectors and other important cats Chester might have already replaced with those taxa clones he made," Mischief said.

Xander swallowed at hearing one of his worst fears stated aloud.

Overhead, thunder boomed and even though he thought it was impossible, the walls seemed to shake with the violence of the storm.

A check of his collar for information on the weather and proximity of the approaching hurricane only told him that he could not connect with Catamondo's satellite system, but it didn't tell him if this was due to the weather or being in a basement. For that matter, purranoid as Chester was, when this safe area had been built, he might have had something put in to block Catamondo from observing what he did down here.

Xander looked around, wondering just how much time Chester had spent down here and if he had left any written clues about his plans. The best way to answer those questions was to read the papers on the table. With that in mind, the three of them divided up the information and began to read.

After a long silence, Mischief looked up and asked, "How many Purrtectors are there?"

Xander blinked as he tried to change his thoughts from understanding DNA to something that should be simple. Unfortunately, he didn't know the answer. "I'm not sure. Why do you ask?"

"Because I don't know and it seems like there should be more than two-hundred-forty-three."

"How did you come up with that number?" Sharkey asked.

"That's how many Purrtectors were getting those cute toys."

She was correct, two-hundred-forty-three seemed low. There were at least two Supreme Purrtectors on each of the six inhabited continents, that was twelve, plus under each Supreme Purrtector, there were either state or regional Purrtectors and in areas that had a large urban population, there were often even special Purrtectors for a city, many of which had Sub-Purrtectors. Now that he was thinking this through, Xander suspected that if all levels of Purrtectors were included, there were far more than two-hundred-forty-three Purrtectors in North America alone.

Mischief shoved the document she had been reading toward him and tapped it with her paw. "He rants about Muffin and Sari and I know you mentioned both of them when we were figuring out the Isla Moreau problem." She flattened her ears. "He also seems to hate Purrsident Mitzi, but it took me a while to figure out that was who he meant because he calls her Ditzy instead of her name." She swished her tiny tail. "That got me wondering how many Purrtectors there were and why he was mailing boxes to two-hundred-forty-three, when

I'm pretty sure that Professor Meowingtons said there were five-hundred Purrtectors in the Caribbean, though only ten were prominent enough to be well known."

"Seriouslys?" Mars said. "Theres mores thans twos Purrtectors?"

"Many more than two," Xander said. "If I were planning on ruining Catamondo by using plague infested toys, I would send them to main Purrtectors, but not the top ones and I would send them to high population areas."

"You could have something there," Sharkey said. "Mumbai is a big city, isn't it?"

"Mumbai is the most populated city in India. In fact it is the eighth most populous city in the world," Mischief said. "And Ms. Sari is Mumbai's Supreme Purrtector."

Sharkey blinked. "Wow, your Professor Meowingtons is thorough."

Mischief shook her head. "I didn't learn that from her. Ms. Fluffy got information from Ms. Sari when we were trying to solve the problem at Isla Moreau."

Sharkey looked at him for confirmation, so he nodded in agreement, even though he didn't like Mischief's continuing use of the word 'we' in regard to his investigation.

The entire house gave a violent groan. Xander looked up and wondered if the hurricane winds had arrived.

"How many Purrtectors are in Mumbai?" Sharkey asked.

Xander frowned. "I'm not sure, but there are over eighteen-million cats, so there must be a lot of them under Sari."

Mischief nodded. "There are seven main areas of that city because it was originally seven different islands. Can you imagine that? Seven islands that turned into cities then somehow became one humongous city?"

"It boggles the mind," Sharkey said.

"Why did you ask how many Purrtectors were in Mumbai?" Xander asked.

"Because most of the toys were being sent to Purrtectors in that city, but none of them were going to Ms. Sari, I thought that was odd, until I realized she was probably too important to distribute them."

For the first time, he realized that his collar had collected the shipping information and forwarded it to Merlin, Fluffy, Purrsey and the professor, but he'd never taken the time to read it. Now, with the house creaking and groaning above them and the wind sounding like a sledgehammer, it seemed like a very good time to sit back and analyze that information along with the new data in front of him. The lights flickered. Realizing that they might lose power or worse, Xander had his collar quickly scan the documents and added them to a file which would automatically send copies of all new information to Merlin and Fluffy as soon as his collar had a signal.

Then, he sat down with Sharkey and Mischief to read the information. He was going over the formula for Mr. M's Special Blend, which was apparently Chester Moreau's recipe for the yummy smelling catnip, and wondering if he was dense, because in all his five years, he'd assumed that catnip was catnip and he'd never realized there was more than one type, much less that there were recipes to blend the herb. When, suddenly, the noise of the wind beating the house was punctuated by the sound of breaking glass and the human cursing.

Mischief stared, round eyed, at the ceiling.

Sharkey tilted her head as she turned to Xander. "Do you think the woman dropped something or is the storm starting to break the house?"

"Whats womans?" Mars asked.

"The only one we saw," Sharkey said. "She was driving the loader-backhoe."

"Thats as mans."

"How would you know?"

"Hows yous thinks Iss gets ins this hous?"

"But the hair is long."

Xander motioned to the papers. "You can argue anatomy later, while we still have light to read, we need to get as much information as possible."

"I never heard a human use that kind of language," Mischief said. "Only Dickens and Rascal when they fight."

"Well, plenty of humans talk that way," Xander said. "Now, can we get to work?"

"Do you think Chester and Damon brewed up this storm because they know we snuck into their house?"

Surely the kitten couldn't be serious, but if he was any good at reading expressions, she was. "No. I think what we're listening to is Hurricane Catarina, which your Professor mentioned when we spoke to her."

"She said it was a tropical storm and that she thought it would head North."

"Even your dear Professor can make mistakes. Because it has obviously moved West."

"Are we gonna die in this hole?"

"No! In fact this is probably the safest place we could have found."

"Then how come Chester and Damon left? If this is so safe, wouldn't they have stayed here?"

"Purrhaps they didn't check the weather," Xander said.

"Or purrhaps they figured they were weather-proof," Sharkey said.

"Ors maybes theys dones heres."

"Probably all three," Xander said, as the lights flickered and then went out. He waited for them to come back on, but they didn't.

Mischief huddled against him and her trembling told him she was crying and he felt Mars curl himself over his collar, but if Sharkey made a sound, he couldn't hear it over the noise of the storm. In fact, the storm had gotten so loud that he wasn't sure he could hear a noisy Haitian tap-tap bus over the racket. With nothing else to do, he lay down and tried to relax.

"Whats your dos?" Mars asked so softly that only he could hear.

"Resting and keeping my strength up, since there isn't much else I can do."

"Trues." Mars sighed. "Toos bads about Mz Lucys."

"What do you know about her?"

"Shes deads."

"How?"

"Flus. Worses, Chesters pluckes hers, thens throws hers outs likes trashes."

"How did you find that out?"

"Iss hears Vi-Purrs talkings. Theys scaredes ofs Chesters and glads theys they don'ts havef furs.""

"I'm glad you told me, but for Mischief's sake, can we act like we don't know what happened to her aunt?" The last thing he needed was for his apprentice to break down crying and lose sight of their mission.

"Yess."

Wrapping his paws around Mischief, Xaner listened to the storm, as she slept.

Chapter 7

Each time he woke up, the storm was still raging and it remained as black as the inside of a coal mine. Despite the temptation to use his collar's LED function, it was more important to conserve power, so he left it off. Fortunately, they weren't in the open barn or up the tree. Unfortunately, without power, he wasn't sure how they would be able to get out of the basement if the hurricane ever moved on, but he was beginning to wonder if the storm was anchored on top of the house.

They stayed in the dark for hours, as the wind and rain beat against the building above. Several times, it sounded like things were breaking. Worse, a damp smell suggested water was seeping into the basement. Xander wondered if the water was coming down from the roof, or if this meant that the roof had broken, or torn off. He sank his claws into the wooden tabletop, so he couldn't flick on his collar's LED function and confirm water was migrating into their sanctuary. While he couldn't control nature, he could control his collar's power usage and it stood to reason that this storm would eventually end. When that time came, he would certainly need his collar for greater things than confirming the damage and a leak.

He wished he could calm his mind like Mischief, so he would have energy, if and when this horrible storm passed on, but it was starting to feel like it would last forever. He hadn't realized he was talking aloud or that he could be heard over the noise until Sharkey said, "It's not so much what happens to you. It's how you handle it and what you do."

"True. Muffin's report after the last big blow said there was total chaos and when the relief groups brought in food, it was gone within seconds. She said people were literally snatching it out of other people's arms." He shivered at the thought of how humans could act.

"They can be barbaric, but they can be wonderful, too. I particularly like Benito Juarez, who said, 'Between individuals, as between nations, peace means respect for the rights of others.'"

It was unusual for her to quote the same thing so frequently, but it was a good thought. "You do realize that not everyone in any given group of humans thinks the same way, don't you?"

"Of course, not all cats even agree, but wouldn't it be nice if our staff started thinking and acting like Chief Benito Juarez?"

"Yes."

Overhead, it sounded like the roof was being ripped off and many things were smashing against the floor.

"It's always darkest before the dawn," Sharkey said.

He waited a moment, then asked, "Who are you quoting?"

"Mouse."

"Oh, I thought it was another of you Indian Chief quotes."

"They aren't the only ones that talk good sense... I call it good sense because I think common sense is a stupid phrase because it isn't common at all."

Mischief stretched, then lay very still. "How long was I asleep?"

"Impossible to know," Xander said.

"Will the storm be over, soon?"

"I can't predict that, either. If you can go back to sleep, do so. I'm sure we'll all need our energy in the morning or whenever this thing passes."

This time, when Mischief snuggled against his stomach and he wrapped his paws around her, they both slept.

The next time he awoke, shafts of pale light illuminated slices of the dark basement enough to see that water was puddling on the floor in several areas and dust floated in the still air. The good news was that the ladder was still standing, though the shaft looked like it had broken wood and other things in it. Even better, his collar had picked up a satellite signal and been able to send the stored information to Merlin and Fluffy. He couldn't be sure, but suspected the outgoing transmission might have been what woke him.

He got up so carefully that Sharkey and Mischief continued sleeping. After testing the ladder and assuring himself it was stable, he climbed up to survey the situation and, if the human was not around, have some breakfast. He had been concerned that the secret door would not work without electricity, but discovered that it was askew enough to get a grip on and push open. When he looked out the now cat-size-gap, the study was unrecognizable. Sky had replaced the ceiling and everything that remained was in chaos. The room reminded him of one of the disaster documentaries Mike liked to watch. He stared at the destruction and marveled at the power it had taken to wreck the building.

Dust and debris covered everything. For the first time since waking, his concern for the human changed from if he could get breakfast without attracting attention to if he was okay. The roof appeared to have been ripped off the entire structure, but fortunately the contents of the kitchen cabinet were safe.

But where was the human? Had he gone outside to work? Seeing the way glass from the broken windows and a tree branch were embedded in a wall, for a moment, Xander feared the worst. Since he didn't smell the coppery scent of blood or the odor of death, it was likely that the human had also survived the storm.

He found a can of Decadent Delicacy and though the label was battered, the seal was intact, so he settled down to eat and think. He'd just gotten his first mouthful when he heard a gasp from the bedroom, which he had never properly inspected. Swallowing quickly, he dashed to the room to see who was there.

Sharkey stood in the dust and rubble, staring at the most ornate four-poster cat bed he had ever seen. It must have been magnificent before the hurricane tore the house apart, but it was just a bed and didn't explain why Sharkey was staring at it and looking like she was about to cry. He moved to her side. "What's wrong?"

She blinked several times. "Don't you see it?"

"Ostentatious, but probably comfortable."

"Not the bed! That!" She gestured to the wall, where someone had apparently used their claw to scratch the plaster. 'Whoever reads this I'm DYING – I'm 4 years old and my name is Lucy. I have the flu. All the chickens already died and I don't think I will last much longer. Please know that I tried to do my best, I just hope it was good enough.'

Sharkey's eyes glistened with unshed tears. "When do you think she wrote that?"

Xander shook his head over the waste. "Does it matter?"

A tear rolled down her cheek. "I guess not. It's just that it's so sad."

"What is?" Mischief asked as she came into the room.

"That the house lost its roof and no one can live here," Xander said. Sharkey gave him a nasty look, so he hastened to remind her of Mischief's family connection, "If your aunt is still alive, I don't know what she will do."

"Well, I guess she'll need to go to one of her other places." Mischief shrugged. "She lives in Santiago most of the time, anyway, and since the barns were blown away, there really isn't a lot for her to oversee here."

"Time to eat a good breakfast and decide on our next move," Xander said, as he went back to the kitchen and hoped they would follow.

They did.

By the time they finished eating breakfast, his collar connected with the satellite network and downloaded the latest weather, news and alerts. He focused on the portion, which reported major flooding in the area. His ears perked when he heard the floods had caused many deaths in Haiti and the Dominican Republic. He switched to the human's news link and learned that over a thousand humans were missing, with many times that number in need of emergency food and non-food assistance. In the Dominican Republic, 414 were dead and 274 are missing – all from the town of Jimani. He gulped, as he realized Jimani was the closest town to the chicken farm. They'd been very lucky to find this food and shelter. The download continued to describe the worst flooding, which occurred along a river system that drained the north flank of the Massif de la Salle and in a poorly drained area along the south slope of the hills. It had been days since he had studied Professor Meowingtons' map, but he was ninety-percent certain that the road Chester and Damon would take to transport the tainted toys was near that area.

The question was if that was good news or bad.

"What's wrong?" Sharkey asked.

He told her what the news report said. Sharkey headed toward the pet door, which was hanging on one hinge, to check outside as Mischief gasped. "Do you think Professor Meowingtons is okay?"

"She was in Malpasse not Jimani," Xander said, "so there is every reason to believe she is fine."

Her ears flattened and her tail fluffed with anger. "When we were at the market, you said, Jimani was on the other side of the market. And The Daily Mews was right there in the market. That sounds awful close to me."

"True, but if you recall the map, this farm was about halfway between Malpasse and Jimani. We're fine."

"Yes, we three are, but what about that human and how about Scar?"

Having forgotten all about the rat, Xander blinked. Mars shifted. "Don't you mean four?" he asked Mischief, to distract her from thoughts of the rat. "Mars is fine, too."

Her eyes widened and she looked at his neck and apologized, but then she went right back to her worries about her beloved teacher. Xander had soon heard quite enough. "Mischief, she is a prominent feline and if she were missing, I am certain it would be in the news. It isn't. If it makes you feel any better, I can send her an email."

"She never checks that stuff."

"Fine," he said, quickly changing tactics, "then I'll email Hector."

Sharkey returned. "Everything is sucking mud and both barns were destroyed, even the loader-backhoe was flipped on its side."

Recalling the way wet mud could turn into quicksand, Xander decided they should stay where they were until things were a little drier. "I know it isn't an ideal solution," he said, "but at least we have food and water here and it will give us time to make sure we didn't overlook any evidence."

"What about Scar?" Mischief asked.

"What about him?" Xander said.

"Well, you are the Purrtector, shouldn't you be trying to purrtect him?"

"One, he was a good guy." At least he hoped he was. "Two," he raised his paw to silence the protest he saw burning in her look, "I tried to purrtect him, but he purrferred to eat tainted eggs instead. Even if he survived the storm, I'd have no idea how to save him from any illness he might have gotten from eating those eggs." He leaned down until their noses touched. "I cannot purrtect him from himself and his choices."

"He was a rat, not a cat, so we really don't have responsibility to purrtect him," Sharkey added.

Mischief gave her a mutinous look, but didn't argue.

Standing up, he headed toward the library. "I'm going to see if there's any other information to be found around here." If his worst suspicions about Chester having other taxa or clones alive were true, purrhaps there was an address book or list. Too bad there was no electricity to power up the computer, but from everything he'd seen at Isla Moreau, Chester purrferred to use old-fashioned paper, so purrhaps it was good that circumstances were forcing him to pay attention to them, instead of the cyber files he purrferred.

Before he decided where to begin, his collar indicated he had a message and to his dismay, Mars tapped the play code. Just how smart was that chameleon and how competent was he with Catamondo's technology?

"Hey Pal! What the heck kind of situation have you gotten yourself into this time? And during a hurricane no less. Are you okay? The data download you sent indicated that you'd programmed your collar to send it when possible. Was that because of the weather or did you get yourself into a situation where survival was questionable?

"According to my research – and I'm really wondering about the accuracy of what I've got so far, there could be a couple of those DNA freaks in office." Merlin hissed. "Can't be positive, but there are a couple of cats who seem to have had drastic purrsonality changes.

"I have never been able to find any record of Damon or Chester in Catamondo's records and when I looked over Lucy Fur's, I realized that the original records were put in by some hacker, so I'm busy-busy checking for that in the billions of other records. Strange that Damon or Chester or whichever one of those Moreaus is the head tom, didn't make fake records for themselves when they made them for Lucy Fur. "By the way, did you ever catch up to Ms. Fur? IF so, were you able to confirm that she was a Moreau puppet or if she was actually pro-Catamondo?" Something sounded suspiciously like a tail thump, then Merlin continued, "Looking over her record, it seems like she tries to help and has a soft spot for orphans.... she also seems to like being in front of cameras and microphones. Amazing that none of the catarazzi ever mentioned the odd color and texture of her fur.

"I don't know why I'm chatting on, when I don't know if you are okay. Please get in touch ASAP and let me know what's going on! Later, Pal. Merlin"

Before he did anything else, Xander sent Merlin and Fluffy a joint voice-mail assuring them that he, Mischief and Sharkey had survived the hurricane and were in a place with plenty of food, as they planned their next step. He also added that he had a report from a reliable source that Lucy Fur had gone over the rainbow... assuming DNA experiments could pass into the here-after, like a real cat. For a moment, he debated mentioning the bird flu epidemic and losing Scar, but decided that wasn't information they needed, so instead, he again added a description of the truck hauling the tainted toys and guesstimated the route, then requested that once the shipments were found, they be monitored and disposed of when it was safe to do so.

"Hows comes?" A tiny voice whispurr-lisped into his ear. "Iss bess ifs destroys nows!"

"Not necessarily true," Xander said.

"Say what?" Mischief asked.

"Sorry, I was talking to Mars."

Her ears flattened. "It's rude to exclude others."

"I wasn't trying to, it's just that you didn't hear his side of the conversation."

With a flick of her tail, she turned her attention to sorting through some papers that looked more like blobs of refuse. Thank Hathor he'd found the other papers and had the sense to scan them when he had, because it looked like the hurricane had destroyed most other information.

The next thing he knew, his collar announced a voicemail from Fluffy. "Xander, what are you doing in the middle of a hurricane?" she demanded. "The moron, says that you might have found a big security breach and he thinks he's found a couple Purrtectors that were cloned or whatever those crazy Moreaus do with fur." He sighed. Why did Fluffy and Merlin keep calling each other rude names?

"At first, I thought the moron had been rolling in nip or something, and I was really confused when you mentioned that the most amazing smelling 'nip in creation was involved with free toys. Why are the Moreaus always doing stuff with 'nip and fur? Is it as strange as I think or not? And why are they always seeming to give away 'nip?" Fluffy hissed. "Believe me, I doubt it's because they want to save us all from mosquitoes. Can a cat actually be so mean and nasty that they want to make cats sick and maybe even kill them just for being cats? Are you sure they actually have cat DNA and aren't dogs pretending to be cats or something?" Fluffy hissed, again. "I mean, thinking like that just isn't right. Not right at all. In fact, it's more like the way humans think and Hathor knows it's why we cats need to be so patient in order to train our staff correctly, but you've got enough problems with your 'nip and fur and weather, you don't need me to go on about humans failing to be humane.

"Let me know what I can do for you other than keep track of those boxes and comb through the files you sent. Meows and Purrs, Fluffy"

By afternoon, all three of them were hot and filthy from looking for clues in the rubble. Worse, they hadn't discovered anything new or interesting. Xander declared that it was time to eat.

"You're going to get fat," Mischief said.

"Purrhaps, but tomorrow, we need to leave here and Hathor only knows how long it will be between meals after that."

"There is plenty of food, how come you're worried about future meals?"

"Do you plan to carry those cans?" Xander tilted his head. "I don't."

"It does not require many words to speak the truth. Chief Joseph of the Nez Perce said that and I don't plan to carry any cans, either," Sharkey added.

Before he chose the flavor he wanted, his collar announced another voicemail from Fluffy. "Xander, do you know there's a flood disaster area near you? If your coordinates are correct it's East of you in an area call Massif de la Salle. I'm not sure if that's the name of a county or mountain or a river. Purrhaps all three. Anyway, The Daily Mews had a photo of a cemetery in Jimani that was overrun by gravel and debris when torrential flows of rainwater ran down the northern flank of the Massif de la Salle.

"According to NOAA, rainfall exceeded 19.7 inches across the border areas of Haiti and the Dominican Republic. During the preceding week, in the town of Jimani 10 inches of rain fell in just 24 hours, which is what they say made the river overflow its banks. I figured it was the hurricane, but I guess NOAA is the expert on this. Anyway, the heavy rainfall caused flash flooding and debris has apparently cut off many of the roads in your region, so you might have a lot of trouble getting back. It seems like places close to rivers are the worst off, so it would be a good idea if you could stay away from low lying areas.

Fluffy cleared her throat, then added, "NOAA said that standing water in low areas has created a series of lakes, one of which submerged the town of Mapou. I don't know how big a town that is, but it sounds awful impressive. If you were planning on going to Mapou, don't bother. Apparently, at least seven lakes have appeared where no lakes existed before. I really can't imagine that, but figured I'd better let you know that your mapping feature might have glitches.

"Be safe, Xander. Meows and Purrs, Fluffy"

As he logged off, his excellent hearing detected the sound of an approaching vehicle. A dash to see past the front door, which was hanging askew, confirmed that a tan jeep-type vehicle was bouncing over the driveway. The windscreen was cracked, the hood was dented and a portion of the canvas top was flapping behind. Had the storm done that damage or didn't those humans know how to take care of their vehicle?

Turning, he told Mischief and Sharkey, "Hide!"

"Why?" Mischief asked.

"Humans coming. At least two and I can't tell if there's anyone with them." He darted behind the sofa, which gave him the ability to watch the door plus a nearby shattered window to jump out of, if necessary.

"Why's that important?" Mischief asked, not having moved an inch.

"Just do as I say!" Outside, the engine turned off.

"What if Chester or Damon is in the car?" Sharkey asked from behind the shade of a broken lamp.

That was exactly what he was worried about, but hadn't thought to mention. Fortunately, the possibility of meeting the two huge cats nose to nose was enough to get Mischief to duck under a buffet.

Outside, the two humans were talking about the damaged buildings and voicing concerns about Fernando. Running steps were on the porch and one kicked the broken door the rest of the way in. Xander moved a pace backward to avoid the cloud of dust the new destruction caused. Sneezes were giveaways and until he knew who this pair was and why they were here, he wasn't about to let them know they were being observed.

The first one in kept shouting, "Fernando." Xander concluded that they were looking for the human with the long coils of hair, but that alone didn't mean this pair was okay. After all, Fernando had been employed by the Moreaus, and that was cause for suspicion. When there was no answer, the first one ran through the house, but the second stood in the door. Was the second a guard to assure that no one left, or was he afraid to enter the wind-whipped room or did he sense he was being watched? Xander lowered his lids, until he was peering through slits. Crashes and bangs came from the back of the house, where the first person continued screaming, "Fernando", the humans' panic increasing with each utterance.

If this was an act to assure him their only reason for coming was to find the human, they were doing a good job... Possibly too good of a job.

The one in the back let out a wail of despair. Had they found the man? Xander frowned as he realized he had not done a proper inspection of the bedroom and bathroom because he had hustled Mischief out before she could read the message Lucy had scratched into the wall, which would have put her into a depression or worse. He needed his apprentice to pay attention to the mission; there would be plenty of time to mourn her aunt, later.

Xander tried to understand what the first one was saying, but could not decipher the accent. He understood the panic, though, and wasn't surprised when the second one ran to the first. As soon as they were out of sight, they began making a lot of noise. Had they found the man? If so, now was the best chance they would have to get out of the house undetected. He hopped out from behind the sofa and told Sharkey and Mischief to follow. In a flash, he was across the porch and had jumped into the back seat of the pitiful tan vehicle. Sharkey was right on his tail, but Mischief lagged enough for him to wonder if she was being ornery or if her shorter legs were just that slow.

Mischief scrambled through the open window and glared at Sharkey. "What if Chester or Damon were in the car?" She snorted. "Obviously they aren't here, so why scare me like that?"

The kitten had a valid point. Xander sighed.

"Because they could have been." Sharkey's tail bristled with anger. "And sitting around to find out for certain was dumber than dumb. When you're told to move, you move."

"You aren't the boss of me."

"Thank Hathor for that!" Sharkey whirled to face him. "Why did we leave the house?"

"Because." He swished his tail, unwilling to waste time on idle chit-chat while he reviewed the new option this vehicle had given them.

Mischief growled. "Not a good enough answer."

"Fine, if you want to walk all the way home, hop out and start walking."

"Oh, so you think that these unknown people, who had you so worried, are now fine. Not only fine, but they will take us wherever we wish." Her ears flattened.

"Like I said, if you prefer to walk back to your mother's, go for it." He hopped onto the floorboards to determine if they could all squeeze under the front seats. It would be a tight fit, but possible. "If you want to ride, you and Sharkey get under this seat and I'll get under the other."

"How come you don't need to share?"

"The two of you combined are smaller than me. Now hurry up, I hear them coming." Better yet, by the sound of it, they were carrying something or someone. If he was right, it would be their friend, who probably needed medical attention and that meant they would go to a doctor. Every doctor he was familiar with lived in an urban area, which meant many more options than he now had, but he didn't have time to explain all this to his stubborn apprentice. Instead, he squeezed under the driver's seat and curled into as small a ball as possible. By the sound of it, Mischief and Sharkey were doing the same thing, which was good, because the sound of feet were moving across the porch. He prayed to Hathor that his luck would hold.

The two humans struggled to load Lucy Fur's human into the back seat. The guy's hand flopped within view and looked positively white. A sniff told Xander that there was a combination of plaster and concrete dust involved, which might explain the color of the once pecan-colored skin. It certainly explained his sudden need to sneeze. Putting both paws over his nose, he tried to hold it in. His eyes watered and he held his breath, but still, the sneeze came.

Fortunately, with all the noises the humans were making, as they tried to get the unfortunate Fernando secured, no one noticed.

By the time the driver's weight was pressing him down, Xander had been able to determine that they intended to take Fernando to Malpasse. As the old jeep bounced down the road, the driver's weight added pressure with each bump. It was so bad that Mars moved next to him, instead of staying on his collar and get squished with each rebound of the seat's iffy springs. Xander adjusted his position to be as flat as possible and sneezed a second time. Thankfully, the sound was lost in the noise of the vehicle's questionable muffler and the blaring music. Obviously, whoever owned the jeep did not have a cat to direct them in the proper maintenance of this vehicle's motor or the cleanliness of its interior. He hoped that once they got out to the main road it would be smoother.

Unfortunately, the entire ride to Malpasse was rough, so by the time they arrived at a clinic near the market, Xander felt like he'd just done ten rounds in the kickboxing ring with a master.

As soon as they carried Fernando away, he whispurred to Sharkey and Mischief that it was time to get out. By the time he dragged himself out from under the seat, they were already out and looking dusty, but still far too fresh to have endured the same ride he had. However, he had a reputation to uphold, so he stretched out the aches as much as possible, while his collar pinpointed their location.

"What now?" Mischief asked.

"Now, we head back to The Daily Mews' office to get information about the storm damage and see if we can track that flatbed truck." As soon as Mars climbed back aboard his collar, he hopped out of the car, and headed through the debris-strewn streets toward the market, Sharkey by his side and Mischief trailing behind. The last time he'd been in this area, the sidewalks were packed with humans, chickens and even a pig on a leash; the stalls had been filled with all sorts of food, overlapping conversations and smells from yummy to foul. Today, they were nearly the only ones moving, everything looked as if it was a war-torn disaster area and the only other animals he saw were humans, using a shovel to scoop up dirt onto a rickety cart, and a scrawny dog, with prominent ribs gnawing something unknown. He hurried along.

"I wish my collar had your capabilities," Sharkey said.

"Yours doesn't have mapping?"

She shook her head. "Basic communications, but it's had lousy reception for the past couple days."

"My reception was messed up, too. I suspect there was shielding in that basement, which makes me wonder if they were doing things down there that they didn't want anyone to see." Xander's tail slashed. "If so, then they don't realize that our technology isn't advanced enough to see through buildings, but I must admit that I don't mind if they think it is."

Sharkey laughed. "When all the trees have been cut down, when all the animals have been hunted, when all the waters are polluted, when all the air is unsafe to breathe, only then will you discover you cannot eat money. That's a Cree Prophecy, but I think it's spot on for how dumb some individuals can be."

He made a sound that he hoped she accepted as agreement, but like most of her sayings, he really didn't see whatever correlation she apparently did. "The office should be through here and around the corner." He darted to his left and, as predicted, arrived at the ancient, weathered door. Entering the pet door, he found himself in the midst of tension.

"Massive runoff along the southern flank of the Massif de la Salle was generated by torrential rains, which formed new lakes and modified the landscape by sweeping tons of debris and gravel downstream. The new lakes are shown here in light blue while the dark blue highlights show the extent of the areas affected by landmass movements," said a tom. "A bit wordy, isn't it? You're supposed to be writing for everyone, not just the academics, like my mother."

"Sorry," an unknown voice mewed. "I'll rewrite it."

"Good. If possible, see if you can find a purrspective to write it from."

"Do you have anyone in mind?"

"Anyone whose home or property was affected. If you could find someone whose home is where one of the new lakes is and write about their emotions and how this sotrm has affected them, that would be ideal."

Xander entered the open doorway as Hector finished advising the young white long-hair. "New lakes?" he asked.

Hector turned to face him, his face appearing much older than it had days ago. "Do you have anything to report?"

"Nothing I can verify, except that hurricane force winds ripped apart Lucy Fur's poultry barns and the nearby house."

Hector perked up and even smiled, then he cuffed the white tom's ears. "That's exactly how you do it."

"Are you here for a job?" the white tom asked.

Xander shook his head. "I need to talk to Hector."

"In that case, can I quote you?"

Xander nodded, then turned his attention to Hector. "Can we talk privately?"

As they moved into Professor Meowingtons' office, the white tom began questioning Mischief and Sharkey about the damage they'd seen. Xander hoped that Mischief was wise enough not to blab everything she knew.

Hector ushered Xander into the office. A quick backward glance assured him that Sharkey was chatting with the white cat instead of Mischief. This was a good thing.

"It's bad, isn't it?"

"What is?" Xander asked, "The storm damage?"

"That, too, but whatever you found out at the farm."

Xander nodded. "Very bad." He then got Hector's promise not to put anything into print before the situation was resolved, because he certainly didn't need any cats who were affiliated with the Moreaus, alerted to his investigation. This situation was difficult enough to unravel as it was, he certainly didn't need any of the individuals involved to get more stealthy. Fortunately, Hector understood and was willing to hold off publication.

"The thing that concerns me is that The Dominican Republic doesn't have a Primary Purrtector," Xander said. "And the worst part is that they don't realize it and I can't reveal this."

Hector's whiskers drooped. "That is a problem." The big fluffy gray and black tom began to pace. "Can't the Council say that she's missing due to the hurricane taking out communications and roads and appoint a temporary substitute?"

"I need to do a DNA check of the Council Members before I know they aren't part of some plot."

Hector frowned. "Is it really that bad or are you purranoid?"

Xander sighed. "Probably a bit of both, but they knew Lady Mitzi's schedule enough in advance to send Jacques there to get fur." Xander's tail swished. "How did they know that?"

Hector's strange orangish eyes became large as pumpkins. "I hadn't thought about that." He shivered so much that his long gray and blac fur made him look like a puffball with bright orange eyes. If Purrsey hadn't mentioned knowing Hector and his mother for her entire life, he would want a DNA test for them, too. However, odd as Hector looked, in his bones, he trusted the tom.

Xander cleared his throat. "As a journalist, you know a lot. How much do you know about The Dominican Republic's political system and structure?"

Hector stared at him. "This island isn't that large, so I know quite a bit... Are you suggesting what I think you are?"

"That you cover Lucy Fur's duties until I sort this out and/or her death is confirmed by some other source and you can come out officially as the Acting Dominican Republic Purrtector." Xander gave a decisive nod.

Hector blinked as he sat down, hard. Then, he blinked, again. "But I haven't been through the training program."

Xander arched a brow. "Do you think we learn catch phrases or something?" He shook his head. "We rely on common sense and adhere to Hathor's Directives and I'm betting you either know those or can easily get a copy." Knowing his mother and the education Mischief had gotten, Hector probably had memorized the rules and regulations set down by Hathor years ago. Hector's distracted-looking nod confirmed his theory. "You are smart and capable. Surely you could unobtrusively fill in for her until the situation is officially sorted out."

"What if the Moreaus target me? Try to give me that horrid flu?"

"More likely, they'd try to get some of your fur and make a clone of you that they could manipulate."

"In which case, they wouldn't want the real me around, so again, they'd find some way to do away with me."

"True, but how much different would that be from any other day?" Xander tilted his head. "Granted, that bunch is more organized than the gangs you and I tend to be forced to deal with and they're certainly stranger and more scientific, but accidents happen every day. There aren't any guarantees in life." He leaned close to softly add, "And just think of the exclusive articles you could get... purrhaps even a book."

Hector blinked very fast, then gave himself a shake. "I'll do it! What do I do first?"

"First, we figure out how we can track that flatbed truck and those malicious toys.... Chester and Damon, too, but my priority is making sure that horrid shipment gets destroyed before they can infect anyone."

"That's sensible, but the route that truck should have taken is right through the area that suffered the worst storm damage, so getting around is going to be difficult." His nose wrinkled in thought. "However, I heard about a group that planned to head out there tomorrow to bring food, water and blankets. I think you and I could invite ourselves along."

"I knew you were the tom for this job!" Xander said as he gave Hector a gentle head butt. Hector looked very pleased by the praise, and soon, they had a practical plan for the following day.

Chapter 8

Riding with the relief workers wasn't much better than the trip from the farm, but at least this time, Xander didn't have worn-out springs above him or a chubby human bouncing on him with each bump in the road. He, Mischief, Hector and Sharkey sprawled on top of a huge pile of blankets in the back of the truck and studied the ravaged landscape. Few buildings were as bad as the ones at Lucy Fur's farm, but many had broken windows and damaged roofs. The closer they got to the river, the worse it got.

"How come that building is catywompous?" Mischief asked.

Catywompous? He blinked, then noticed the structure was tilting. Looking around, Xander noticed more buildings, which appeared to have shifted off their foundations, others had collapsed and some, like Lucy's house, were missing roofs. "Apparently either a flood or the wind pushed them off."

"Oh. I should have known that."

Xander nodded. Yes, she should have.

"I guess that I didn't realize the storm was strong enough to move a whole building, but those aren't really that big, are they?" Mischief sighed.

"In town, most buildings have plumbing and power," Hector said, "but many in the rural areas don't have those luxuries."

"Eeeewwww! I can't imagine not having water." Mischief's nose wrinkled, as if she smelled something foul.

Sharkey snickered. "American Indians lived without that for ages, some still do. In fact, they didn't live in houses; they lived in tipis. Luther Standing Bear of the Oglala Lakota Sioux said, 'I am going to venture that the man who sat on the ground in his tipi meditating on life and its meaning, accepting the kinship of all creatures, and acknowledging unity with the universe of things was infusing into his being the true essence of civilization.' Isn't that a wonderful thought – living in kinship with nature? I would love to live in a tipi and experience that!"

"I like where I live now," Mischief said. "I can go swimming whenever I like."

Hector blinked rapidly, then looked at Xander.

Xander sighed. "She has an unnatural obsession with water."

"You're serious?"

Xander nodded. "Check out my humans' boat blog, if you don't believe me. Before we left on this mission, just about every day they blogged about her – and had photos of her boogie boarding and playing in the water."

"And you were okay with that?"

Xander shrugged. "I would purrfer that she devoted as much effort to her other subjects, but admit that my wind surfing skills played a big part in why I was appointed to this position."

"You can see that I am right here, while you're talking about me, right?" Mischief's tail thumped the blanket.

Xander smiled. "Don't worry, you aren't invisible. In fact, your water skills might even be handy in the flood situation."

Mischief sat up straight and told Hector, "I'm really good."

"Better than Xander?"

She snorted. "He avoids the water."

Sharkey and Hector laughed, then Sharkey said, "Most of us do, we cats have a reputation to maintain, you know."

"Very true," Hector said, then turned to Xander. "When do you plan to teach her to surf?"

Mischief got a strange expression on her little calico face and gave him an odd look, as if wondering what Hector knew that she didn't, but wisely kept quiet.

"There hasn't been an opportunity for that and to be honest, I've been trying to figure out a way to have her apprentice with Merlin for a couple weeks."

"Ohhhhh," Sharkey said, "Merlin is amazing. I was so shocked to learn that he wasn't just a pretty boy." Her eyes took on a dreamy look and Mischief looked at her like she'd grown five ears. "I would love to have the chance to meet him and learn his water skills." She turned to Xander. "He's the one who taught you, isn't he?" Xander nodded. "I thought so. Is it true that he can do a handstand while surfing?"

"I haven't seen it, but wouldn't doubt it," Xander said.

"Seriously?" Mischief said. "That cat on the Elegant Eats cans, who advertises Savory Salmon, Chicken Cordon Bleu, and Decadent Delicacy, is not only your buddy, but a Purrtector AND he can surf?" Xander nodded. "Then how come I ended up being apprenticed to you?"

"Because you and I are here and you have the potential to eventually take over as Sea Purrtector, and for now, you have the abilities to be a good apprentice," Xander said. "However, you really do need to get more serious about the other aspects of your education."

She moved until she was nose to nose with him. "I'll make you a deal. If I ace all my classes, you arrange for me to meet Merlin and have him teach me how to surf."

Since Xander had been trying to figure out how to do that, anyway, knowing that Merlin actually loved teaching others to adapt to water, he easily said, "Deal." Then gave her a gentle head butt. "Now, can we focus on the Moreau problem?"

She nodded.

"Good!"

Hector cleared this throat. "Once we arrive in Jimani, I expect this transport to head North, around Lago Enriquillo and on into Baoruco Provence."

Sharkey's head swiveled sharply. "Isn't that more mountainous, so won't there be more landslides?"

"Yes, it's the area with the worst problems, but it also has the best road, so if we can assume that the service truck we're trying to locate took the main route, we should be on the same track." Hector's strange orange eyes closed for a moment and he shook his head, then he looked Xander in the eye. "I heard that the Purrtectors had special collars, and while yours looks rather drab, every once in a while I think I catch it looking at me."

Mischief and Sharkey burst into laughter, but Xander looked around to make sure no human was watching. Then said, "Mars, would you like to be introduced to Hector? Off the record, of course." He gave Hector a stern look as he felt Mars uncoil and sit up. "Hector, you were looking at a trusted associate, Mr. Mars Quatro, who not only is an excellent source of information and intelligence, but is kind enough to use his skills to conceal my collar and rank from those who might wish to thwart my efforts. Mars, I know you are well acquainted with Mr. Meowingtons."

Hectors eyes looked big as navel oranges as he stared at the top of Xander's head and though his mouth was moving, no sounds came out. His obvious stress had Mischief rolling with silent laughter on the bundle of blankets. She vibrated so hard that she rolled right off the blankets, landing on top of an adjacent box.

Sharkey head-butted Hector. "Haven't you ever met a chameleon before? Mars really is a worthy individual." Still apparently dazed, Hector shook his shaggy head so hard that his long tufts of fur shook. Sharkey leaned close and whispurred, "Well, as a journalist, you should consider forming a working relationship with them. They can get into places and remain unnoticed like you wouldn't believe."

Hector smoothed his wild charcoal-gray and black fur as he stared at the top of Xander's head, where Mars was perched. "Innovative idea." He leaned closer. "Are your services tied to Xander or are you for hire?"

"Xanders iss mys friends."

"He is helping us by choice," Xander hastened to add. "If he wishes to accompany us when the mission is done, he's welcome to do so, but if he wishes to stay here and do something else – including work with you – he's also welcome to do that. The choice is his."

"You don't need to decide now," Hector said, "but Mars, my good fellow, you have an open invitation."

"Why are there roofs in that lake?" Mischief asked, as she stared down the hillside.

"Because, last week, it was part of the town," Hector said. "That's one way a flood can look."

"Seriously?" Mischief asked. Hector nodded. "Wow!" She frowned. "Why would humans put all the effort into putting a house where it could get drowned? I mean, I like water and all, but I certainly don't think it's smart to put your house where it could get under water. That would make it impossible to cook and there wouldn't be any air to breathe."

Hector's whiskers swished, but he didn't say anything. Xander couldn't think of anything to say, either.

By the time the truck made its way through Jimani, many of the blankets, bottles of water and boxes of food had been distributed. It turned due North, Lake Enriquillo on their right, hills on their left. In many places, the water covered the road so a human in tall black rubber boots and carrying a long stick would get out of the cab and walk ahead of the truck.

"Why does he do that?" Mischief asked.

"Purrhaps he's looking for alligators," Sharkey said.

Mischief's nose turned white. "Alligators?"

"More likely he is checking how deep the water is," Xander said. "Engines and motors don't work in deep water."

Mischief snorted. "If that was so, submarines wouldn't work."

He resisted the urge to hiss, and said, "Unless they are designed to be waterproof, they do not work."

Sharkey nodded in agreement. "He's right. For one thing, they are made of metal and when that rusts, which quickly happens in water, they don't work right."

To his utter disgust, Mischief appeared to accept Sharkey's comment, without question.

Through the day, the truck continued to follow the road, often stopping to clear debris out of the road, or cautiously go through water. Many times they stopped to give more supplies to storm survivors. The curving road eventually turned Southeast, then Eastward, and then North-northeast, but no matter which way the road twisted, Lago Enriquillo with debris from the storm floating on its water and heaps of rubble on its shore lay to their right.

Finally, as the setting sun heated his back, the truck ground to a halt and the driver turned off the engine. Xander stood up so he could see ahead. To his surprise, the way was blocked by shrubs, dirt and rocks. One of the rocks blocking their way was larger than the truck's cab. His seal-point coat stood on end as he thought about the kind of power it would take to move so much earth onto the road.

"I've heard about landslides," Sharkey said, as she gazed upward at the mountainside on their left, "but I never imagined how much could actually move. Do you think the hurricane did that?"

"What else could have?" Mischief asked.

"It was probably due to the rain," Xander said, as he looked for a way around the mess, which appeared to go from the fresh rip in the steep mountainside on his left to where the rubble ended in the lake on his right.

Sharkey scratched her ear. "Now what?"

Hector sighed. "Apparently, we walk."

"If we're lucky, vehicles coming from the other direction will be stuck on the other side," Xander said. "Surely someone will turn around and go back."

"Hide!" Mischief gasped as she dove behind a box.

Xander and Sharkey jumped down, but Hector, who wasn't a trained Purrtector, merely sat up, a startled look on his face. Xander peeked up at him in time to see one of the Vi-Purrs fly low over the truck. "Get down here," he hissed. This time, Hector moved. Xander hoped it wasn't too little, too late.

"Do you think they saw us?" Mischief meowed.

"Who?" Hector asked.

"Clade and Allele – also known as the mutant Vi-Purrs, I told you about them," Xander said.

"The Chupacabras?" Hector said. "Zounds, this is a mega scoop." He jumped back onto the blankets, but Xander yanked him back.

"Think about what you've heard about what Chupacabras do to their victims," Xander hissed, "then ask yourself if they will kill you on sight or take the time for an interview."

"But you're here to back me up."

"Do you think I'm going to endanger myself, Mischief and Sharkey because you're too focused on a story to purrtect yourself?" Xander flattened his ears. "If you think that, think again."

"Mr. Hector, you're the Acting Dominican Republic Purrtector, you need to behave like it," Mischief said.

Hector's orange eyes focused on his apprentice and for a brief moment, Xander feared that he would smack her, then Hector gave his shaggy head a shake. He hoped that the big tom had realized the story was a situation, not just a story. Hector ducked low. "What do you suggest?"

"First, we watch to see what they're doing," Xander said.

"Do you think they're landing there because they know we need to cross there on foot?" Mischief asked.

"If they wanted to grab us, I think they would have attacked us right here," Sharkey said.

"I agree," Xander said, "They might not be the most intelligent beings, but surely they must realize that if they could see us, we could see them, so it doesn't make sense to think that attacking us is their goal." Then again, their eyes are on top of their heads, which was very peculiar. So while they had been visible to anyone looking up, they might not be able to look below very well. He carefully rose so he could peer over the box, but he couldn't see Clade and Allele anywhere. Had they landed? They had certainly been flying low enough.

The doors for the truck slammed shut and he watched the two humans walk toward the landslide.

Was it coincidence that Clade and Allele had arrived moments after he had?

And why were the humans leaving?

"We need to get out of here," he said, as he dove over the back of the truck, which was the farthest away from the landslide, then darted into the weeds between the road and lake. Hector rushed a bit too fast and nearly tumbled down the steep bank which ended in the water. Xander narrowed his eyes as Mischief approached, certain that if she fell in, it wouldn't be an accident. Fortunately, she ducked into the tall grass next to Sharkey and became still as the heavy, afternoon air.

Xander sniffed the air and caught the vague, but unmistakable scent of Mr. M's Special Blend. He blinked in surprise.

Was the truck close?

If not, how long did the fragrance linger?

Did the Vi-Purrs smell the same as Mr. M's Special Blend?

Or were they following the scent?

He carefully breathed in the air from several directions and realized that the aroma was coming from the general area where the Vi-Purrs had been heading. A kernel of hope blossomed as he theorized that Clade and Allele had been attracted by the enticing odor and were not tracking him.

Could the truck be close by?

"Iss possibles," Mars said. "Iss goes sees." In a flash, he leaped free and moved faster than Xander would ever have believed such short legs could travel onto the road, then with a leap and a bound, he was on the landslide, heading up, through a crevasse. Then, in a flash, he disappeared.

"That was disconcerting," Hector said. "Why did he run away?"

"Mr. Mars doesn't run away," Mischief hissed. "He collects information."

Hector gave her a confused look, but wisely stayed silent.

As the shadows lengthened, Xander heard the two humans shouting. Had they spotted Mars? It seemed doubtful that they would make such a fuss over one small chameleon, but when the Vi-Purrs exploded into the air, their shouts were understandable. "Don't move," he hissed at Hector, who had straightened to get a better look.

"But those are the Chupacabras!"

"And they love to kill," Xander said. "Is this story worth your life?"

"Are those spines on their backs?"

"Yes, and their eyes are like crocodiles' and their wings are sort of like bats, but I have it on good authority that their bite is poisonous because they were mainly created with snake and cat DNA. Now will you please hide?" he hissed.

Hector ducked down, but was so excited that he began whispurring about Chupacabras and telling him how the legends were wrong, because they certainly were not the size of a pig. He smacked Hector when he started to sit up, a second time.

"I'm beginning to wonder if you have enough sense to be a Purrtector. It doesn't matter if they have rough-looking bellies that look like scaly brown mud, which could either mean they needed a bath or that they simply have nasty skin. Those long, pointy crocodile-like teeth can rip flesh apart and they can tuck in their big bat-like wings and swoop down like a bolt of lightning, so do you really want to make yourself its target?"

"You're right, their eyes are like a crocodile's," Mischief added, "so they probably didn't notice Mr. Hector when they took off, but they sort of tilt when they fly, so they can see down and movement is really easy to see. That's why Mr. Xander wants you to stay still."

Hector closed his eyes and seemed to focus on breathing.

As if reacting to his thought, one of them angled its serpentine body downward, tucked the big bat-like wings close around its body and dove. A chill rippled over Xander, even though he could see that it was diving toward the lake, instead of him. He tapped his collar to begin recording the creature as the long sinuous form cut into the water like an arrow. Behind him, Sharkey gave a soft gasp, but it was drowned out by the shouts of the humans.

Moments later, as the second Vi-Purr dove into the lake, the shrieking sound of metal being forced burst from the direction the humans were at. With Clade and Allele both under water, it was time to move. "Follow me," Xander said, as he darted in the direction of the human voices. Before the Vi-Purrs' long, pointy snouts emerged from the water, the four of them were safely in the shadows of a car-size boulder, which was half-buried in the debris on top of the landslide. Having something solid at his back was comforting.

"They swim weird," Mischief whispurred.

Xander pressed his head against hers and breathed. "They swim like snakes and need I remind you how well sound travels over water?"

Mischief's nose was so close to his ear that it sounded like a motor when she exhaled. "How could they possibly hear us over those humans?"

She had a point, but one could never predict when background noise would stop. Strangely, the humans sounded like they were getting closer, even though he hadn't moved so much as the tip of his tail since ducking into the rock's shadow.

A glance at the lake told him that the VI-Purrs were both swimming toward him and each had a flapping fish clenched in its crocodile-like teeth.

What did they eat besides fish? If they had either serpent or crocodile DNA, they probably even ate cats. A new chill rushed from the tips of his chocolate ears to the end of his bristling tail. Silently, he watched the Vi-Purrs swim toward him, and listened to the humans, who also seemed to be getting closer. Of the two potential problems, he knew Clade and Allele were by far the worst, so he zeroed in on them and nearly heaved a sigh of relief when they began climbing onto a slab of stone, which was half-submerged in the lake.

Once the worry that they were coming toward him dissolved, he realized that the humans were now very close. Their voices were strained and they sounded like they were gasping for breath, but he kept his attention on the Vi-Purrs until they were both on top of the rock and their attention was obviously on the still-wriggling fish.

"Isn't that the same human who was driving the freight truck?" Mischief breathed into his ear.

Slowly, so his movement didn't attract attention, Xander turned his head to study the trio approaching him. Three? The one in between was being half carried toward the truck he'd arrived on. Though he looked horribly bloody and unable to walk unaided, he was nearly positive Mischief was correct about the injured one's identity.

If the Vi-Purrs were here and the driver they had been searching for was here, could it possibly mean the truck – and more importantly, its cargo – was nearby? He didn't realize he'd whispurred the thought aloud until Mischief said, "That's exactly what I was wondering."

While Mischief and Sharkey watched the approaching humans, Xander studied Clade and Allele, who seemed to be struggling to stay on top of the big rock. Previously, they had appeared to be swift, skillful climbers, but he'd only had one opportunity to see them scale a tree. Perhaps rocks were more difficult to sit on or maybe they'd climbed the tree so many times that they'd perfected a way to wrap their tails around the trunk for balance. Regardless, the effort to sit on top of the rock while controlling a flopping fish seemed to be difficult for them. Purrhaps they weren't as intimidating an adversary as he had originally assumed.

They certainly weren't as coordinated.

And by the time the one sprawled on the rock to eat, it was moving slow and appeared to have difficultly holding onto the injured fish.

Xander narrowed his eyes and recalled the symptoms for bird flu: fever, cough, sore throat, and nausea, which often progressed to severe breathing problems, including pneumonia and acute respiratory distress syndrome. Unfortunately, it was impossible to determine if either of them had any of the symptoms, but the way they were moving and the fact that Lucy Fur had been reportedly infected made it seem possible.

Maybe even likely.

The trio of humans shuffled past their rock and helped the injured one lie down in the back of the truck on the blankets they had ridden on. One got into the cab and started the engine, while the other remained in the back and offered the injured one a drink. Coughing and choking, he guzzled it as the truck did a three point turn and headed back where it had come from.

Mischief snuggled close and shivered. Xander bent close to her ear and whispurred. "We'll be fine. After all, this is where we need to be."

"But we'll need to sleep outside."

"Our ancestors did it for generations."

"What if those Chupacabras eat us in our sleep?"

"They look scary," he said, "but they can barely manage those fish. I'm pretty sure we can take them, if it becomes necessary."

"B-b-but wh-what if Damon and Chester are also h-here? I m-mean, you said that you s-s-smelled Mr. M's Special Blend, too. And you admitted that if that human was h-here, the truck probably was, t-too."

"True. But did you notice anything different about Clade and Allele from the first time we watched them?"

Her little calico face scrunched up in thought, then he saw the sudden change when she realized what he had noticed. "They were unbalanced and might be sick!"

"Exactly."

"Do you think Damon and Chester might be sick, too?"

"They were traveling with the infected toys, and someone had to have packaged them. I doubt it was your aunt." He refrained from pointing out how unlikely he thought it was for her to pluck out her own infected feathery fur to decorate and package the toys or mentioning the message clawed into the wall.

"So you think Clade and Allele packaged them?"

"There are only five options that I'm aware of and they're two of them. The fact that they are moving slowly and neither of them seems to be able to control an injured fish makes me think they have that flu." He watched as the Vi-Purr, which had dropped its catch, made a feeble attempt to get the fish away from its taxa. The result was that the second fish managed to flip away and fall off the rock, just as the first one had. What was most interesting was that neither Vi-Purr seemed to have the energy to go after them, or even fight each other over their loss. In fact, both of them simply sprawled on the slab of rock and appeared too tired to do anything but bask in the lengthening rays of afternoon sun.

"Chief Joseph of the Nez Perce said, 'We live, we die, and like the grass and trees, renew ourselves from the soft earth of the grave. Stones crumble and decay, faiths grow old and they are forgotten, but new beliefs are born. The faith of the villages is dust now... but it will grow again... like the trees.'" Sharkey's delicate black and white face was watching the Vi-Purrs with a sorrowful expression.

"You think they're sick or maybe they're on a diet?" Mischief asked.

Huh? Xander motioned for her to explain.

"Well, why else didn't they eat their fish?" She frowned. "Mr. Xander figures that means they're sick or something. Do you agree?"

Sharkey nodded. "The only other thing I can think is that the fish didn't taste good, but they move like they don't feel good, so I'd bet sick."

Hector sighed, "I wish I could write about this. A photo of that pair would guarantee me front page and international exposure. Just look at them, will you! They remind me of the a feline Frankenstein."

"And as soon as this mission is over, you will have plenty of information and photos to publish several articles." Xander tapped his collar to stop recording, then sent a copy to Merlin and Fluffy and saved it to his cloud. Once this mission was over, he would send a copy to Hector, but he didn't dare do that, yet, because he didn't know if the tom had any assistants who might access his email and take it upon themselves to publish the clip.

"If they're so sick, we should attack them," Mischief said.

Sharkey's golden eyes went wide as she glanced at him. Xander swished his tail and asked, "What is the main thing we need to do when we approach an unknown situation?"

"Ascertain the situation, while keeping a low profile," Mischief said.

Sharkey visibly relaxed, but Hector's ears perked in obvious interest.

Xander inclined his head. "So you did pay attention." He had wondered, particularly when he realized she wasn't turning in her homework or participating in online discussions.

"Of course I pay attention to stuff that's important," she hissed. "So shouldn't we look for that truck, now, while they aren't looking so good?"

"The humans obviously found the chauffeur." Xander looked her straight in the eye. "Do you remember if he was alone, when we saw him?"

Mischief's leaf green eyes went wide a moment before her calico fur stood on end. "He was with D-Damon and Ch-Ch-Chester."

Xander nodded. "Still think we should all rush over there?" She shook her head. "That's what I thought, but after moonset, I shall do a reconnaissance and see if the truck is nearby and if I can figure out what happened to them. In the meantime, I intend to wait here and see if Mars returns with information."

"Don't you mean moonrise?"

"I'm pretty sure I mean moonset." He narrowed his eyes at Mischief. "Do you remember the moon cycle?"

"If the left side of the Moon is dark then the light part is growing, so the Moon is getting bigger. If the right side of the Moon is dark we're heading toward dark nights."

Xander nodded. "Do you remember what the moon looked like last night?"

Her nose scrunched in thought. "I think it was dark on the left, and almost half and half."

"Very good. So when does the moon rise, when it is dark there?"

She shrugged.

"Purrhaps she hasn't gotten to that lesson," Hector said. "Fortunately, I always post this in The Mews and I can tell you that the moon rose at 11:31 this morning and it will set at 22:57 this evening." Mischief looked up at the sky, doubt and surprise in her expression. "Trust me, it's up there, you just can't see it because the sun is too bright."

"If you say so."

Xander nodded at Hector. "He is correct and once it sets, the shadows stop shifting, so that is when I will check the situation. For now, we need to rest." He set his collar to give a silent alarm if there was movement within fifty feet, then got comfortable and began to meditate. As was her custom, Mischief snuggled against his stomach. One of these days, he needed to cure her of this habit, because if he needed to respond to danger, she would be in his way.... but not today. Today had been stressful and despite the fact that Clade and Allele were in full sight, their eyes were closed and it looked like they were too sick to do much of anything other than take a nap.

Shortly after midnight, Xander got up, making certain not to wake Mischief. Sharkey's eyes opened and her ears perked, but he signaled her to be quiet and stay where she was. Though her ears flattened, she did as instructed. On paws quiet as the shadows he blended into, Xander followed the faint scent of Mr. M's Special Blend and eventually found the truck on its side and half-buried at the edge of the landslide. Hathor's timing had been excellent. If the vehicle had been moving faster, it would have escaped. As it was, the truck and its lethal contents had effectively been captured, thus saving countless cats from the potential plague. He sat still as the surrounding land, watching the truck and wondering what his best option was for destroying the contaminated toys.

As he silently studied the situation, his collar let him know there were three life-signs nearby. One was strong, but the other two were faint. Fortunately, none of them seemed to be approaching his position.

Yet.

A faint breath of wind brought the mingled aromas of Mr. M's Special Blend and gasoline. Despite the rankness of the petrol, his mouth watered with the lure of the diabolical blend Chester had come up with.

For security's sake, all Purrtectors were part of the fifty percent of cats who didn't have the gene that made them susceptible to herb addiction.

Yet he felt the lure.

How had Chester managed that? And what diabolical chemistry had he used in this plot to undermine Catamondo?

There was a rustling movement near the front of the truck, but the only actual thing he saw was some dirt dribbling downward.

Xander carefully sniffed the air. Was it his imagination or did he also smell bad eggs, old blood and rotting fish? If he hadn't been so concerned about the herb's influence overpowering him, he would have been offended by the unfortunate mixture of smells.

A tickle at the back of his neck almost caused an involuntary scratch response, but his extensive training allowed him to remain still. The next moment, a familiar voice whispurr-lisped a greeting into his ear.

Why hadn't his collar picked up Mars' approach?

And why did his collar still state that all three of the life signs were still in the truck, when one was obviously around his neck?

He would need to speak to the development team about this! However, Mars was an excellent spy and he was delighted to have him back. Xander continued watching the wrecked truck, yet relaxed as Mars reported that Damon and Chester had both been seriously injured in the crash. Damon had been propelled into the windscreen, suffering head and spine injuries, which probably meant his life sign was one of the faint ones. Apparently, Chester had also suffered a spinal injury, so his back legs couldn't move properly and when the Vi-Purrs had landed, they had burrowed into the cab and attacked Chester, though Mars wasn't sure why they had done that.

Pity squeezed his heart for a moment, before he reminded himself that they had intentionally infected Lucy Fur, then used her infected feather-fur to contaminate irresistible toys, which they were sending out by the thousands. His ears flattened with irritation.

Are their injuries why the humans left them and only helped the human?

"Parts. Damons iss toos bigs toos gets outs windows, buts Iss donts thinks theys likes cats."

Xander peered at the truck and realized a large rock was partially covering the area where he suspected the door would be.

Damon had gotten into the truck, first, Chester second. Purrhaps Damon was even on top of Chester, which could mean Chester was the other faint life sign. But why three life-signs?

"Was there anyone else there?"

"Scars."

The rat was here? He'd been certain he either died of overeating or bad food. Amazing that he'd not only survived his appetite, but a hurricane. "How did he get there?"

"Yous didn'ts sees hims sneaks onto thes trucks?"

"At the barn?"

"Yess!?"

"No, I didn't." Why had the rat done that? While Xander could understand the lure of food, he didn't think that Mr. M's Special Blend would tempt a rat, but it could be one reason why Scar had chosen to leave with the shipment of contaminated toys. Of course, there were other reasons, too, but he didn't want to believe that Scar had gone to help his taxa.

As the first rays of light brightened the horizon, his acute hearing picked up the sounds of the VI-Purrs waking. Unless he wanted eyes in the sky watching when he did a visual inspection of the cab, he needed to move now.

Silent as the stars lingering above, he leaped onto the big rock above the boulder holding the door shut, then sprawled on top of it and inched forward until he could see down through the broken window. A foul stench made him gag, so he held his breath. Eyes watering, he peered down at the crumpled bodies below. They didn't look scary enough to have come up with an evil plan to undermine Catamondo. In fact, they looked pitiful.

"You should leave before the smell overcomes you."

He sat back and turned to come face to face with Scar. "I thought you were dead."

"Why would you think something like that?"

His tail lashed in frustration, before he managed to control it. "You ate contaminated eggs for one thing, never returned for another. And they put all those eggs in a hole."

Scar smiled. "Being buried with a feast like that would have been wonderful!" Xander blinked and reminded himself that he was dealing with a rat, which obviously had a very different grasp on what was smart, from what a rational cat would. "Besides, I'd been vaccinated against that plague, so it was no problem for me to eat those eggs, but I wouldn't recommend it for you or the ladies." Having never thought of Mischief as a lady, and rarely even recalling that she was a female, Xander blinked some more. Scar peered over the edge of the rock and hissed. "Of course, the holier than thou ones didn't realize I'd switched the phony shot they intended to give me for the real vaccine and that they gave each other the placebo." His snicker sounded evil. "That's why I knew it was safe for me to eat that banquet and I also knew they could get the flu that they wanted everyone else to get." Scar's whiskers bristled and his eye gleamed in the rising sun. "Divine justice is what I planned, and I'd just chewed through a box and got out a few contaminated feathers to infect them when the whole truck went topsy turvy."

"Another sort of divine justice?" Xander asked.

"Guess you could look at it that way, but I would have liked watching them get sicker and sicker."

"And you don't think that is happening?"

Scar scratched his ear. "Maybe, but not like I intended."

"Sometimes fate has other plans." Xander sighed. "When I took off chasing this truck, I didn't expect to find this and now I realize the problem has changed."

"How so? I mean, it looks like the landslide took care of a lot of things for you."

"True, but if any cat happened by, they would be attracted to those toys, get sick and continue the problem. So, I need to figure out how to get rid of them."

Scar smirked. "I've already been working on that."

"How so?"

"Smell the petrol?"

He'd been trying not to smell the gasoline, but it was awfully strong. "Of course."

"I planned to burn those things to a crisp."

"Why?"

"They are bad."

"For cats and kittens, not you!"

"You think I don't care about others? You think I want to live with the knowledge that some of my taxa were so evil-minded that they wanted to make others ill just to make themselves feel superior or powerful or smarter or why-ever they did this? Lucy was my furiend." Scar's eyes seemed to shimmer with unshed tears. "If she was your taxa and furiend, would you want to sit by and let someone kill her, then use her to destroy others or would you try to stop it?"

"I would try to stop it."

Scar sadly nodded. Just then an ear-splitting shriek made his fur stand on end. He whirled to look at the rock where Clade and Allele had let the fish get away and then slept. One of them was awake and screeching at the sky, but the other one appeared to be sleeping. How could anything sleep through that racket? He keyed his collar to verify life signs and it quickly came back with the information he suspected – only one of the Vi-Purrs was alive. He watched the one remaining rant and howl its loss and anger.

"Poor Clade. Allele was his only real family and furiend. Now, he's even more alone than me," Scar said.

Xander blinked in surprise. "You can tell them apart?"

Scar nodded. "I figure Allele had a worse case of that flu. It's good Chester isn't in a position to use his body for some nasty plan." Scar adjusted the prism so the rising light was perfectly magnified onto the spilled fuel. "We need to get away from here before it ignites."

"Good idea. I'm sure the others have woken and wonder where I am."

"They're here, too?"

Xander nodded as he hopped down. "Sharkey, Mischief, Hector and I were trying to find this truck so we could make sure those toys didn't get passed out."

"Why'd you bring Hector?"

Knowing how much the rat adored Lucy Fur, it wasn't easy to tell him the information he'd learned about her, but he also needed to be honest. "Ms. Lucy hasn't been seen in weeks, so I needed to appoint someone to oversee her duties until we can find out what happened to her."

"You think she's dead."

"It's a possibility. After all, she was at a bird farm, where there was a bird flu epidemic and you did say that some of her DNA came from a macaw."

Scar sighed. "True. Fact is, I know she's dead, but I hate to think it was because of Gabby's DNA. Gabby was a good bird and didn't deserve what happened to her any more than me or Lucy." When Clade launched himself toward the dimming stars, Scar ducked into the shadows.

So did Xander.

Had Clade seen them? Xander swallowed and waited to see what the Vi-Purr intended to do.

Overhead, there were several more cries, as he circled the sky. Was Clade riding a wave of air or watching the ground for movement? Xander was torn between racing to let the others know he was fine and the certainty that if he ran, he would surely be spotted. The last thing he wanted was for Clade to notice him, particularly now, when he was obviously upset and might want to take his loss and rage out on someone.

"Iss cans goes. Tells Miss Mischiefs yous iss goods," Mars whispurred into his ear.

"Thanks, but I can't ask you to do that." It had always been his opinion that he could not ask or worse – order – someone to do something he was unwilling to do."

"Iss smalls ands sames colors as dirts. Hes nots sees mes." With that, Mars leaped onto the ground and quickly disappeared into the shadows. It was downright amazing how fast the chameleon could move when he chose to. Almost as amazing as how he seemed to vanish.

Xander cautiously looked back at Scar, whose whiskers were trembling as he stared wide-eyed at Clade, who continued circling and screeching his pain and loss to all who would listen. With a flick of his claw, his collar added pictures of the truck and its passengers to the growing cloud file, along with visuals of Allele's body and Clade's rage. His attention focused on Allele. If he had died of some strain of bird flu, he might present a danger to others. Possibly even cats. He didn't know what he could do, particularly while avoiding actual physical contact, but he knew that as a Purrtector, it was his responsibility to purrtect others and that meant he needed to do something about Allele.

Just not while Clade was watching.

Chapter 9

As the rising sun peeked above the horizon and the shadow he was camouflaged in shortened, Xander noticed a tendril of smoke rising into the air. Was Scar's plan actually working? Would the truck catch fire and, if it did, would the lethal toys burn?

And if they burned, would the smoke be harmful?

He forced himself not to shiver because he knew that movement was an easy thing for predators to zero in on and he didn't need Clade attacking him – at least not before he had a plan.

A tiny flame flared.

Scar made a sound of satisfaction.

Clade continued screeching his pain to anyone who would listen.

Abruptly he felt a familiar thump on his neck, which announced Mars' return. "Theys iss goods, toos. Ands theys says bees carefuls."

"Thanks, my friend," Xander whispurred.

"Misters Hectors wants tos knows ifs Alleles deads ofs birds flus."

"I'm not a doctor, but I think it is safe to assume so."

"Thats whats Iss thinks, toos." Mars shivered. "Yous thinks hes contagious?"

"Again, I don't know, but since Chester used feathers from sick animals to decorate those toys, I assume Allele is a hazard."

"Iss thinks this, toos. Sos does Misters Hectors ands hes says he's Dominicans Purrtectors ands Alleles is in Dominicans ands hes musts fixes."

"It would be too dangerous for him to do anything."

"Whys?"

"If he got the flu, he could give it to others. Trust me, I've been trying to figure out what to do about Allele. I just haven't figured out a plan, yet."

"I've been vaccinated," Scar said.

"I know, but you can't be expected to move something more than ten times your size and while Allele needs to be buried, he's far too big for you to handle." Scar snorted. "He's too much dead weight for me to deal with, too." Xander winced at the unintended pun. "Besides, as long as Clade is flying around in circles and pitching his fit, we can't do anything."

"Tell that to Hector," Scar said.

Xander looked where Scar's attention was and saw Hector slinking toward the huge flat-topped rock, "Idiot!" he hissed, as he moved to cut him off.

Mars jumped away.

Xander pounced on Hector before he was in position to make the leap to the rock. "Hey!" Hector yowled. "What's wrong with you?"

An accompanying scream from Clade made their fur stand on end.

"What's wrong with ME?" Xander hissed. "What's wrong with you?"

"Mars said that Vi-Purr was dead and probably contaminated. Just because I'm only the Acting Dominican Republic Purrtector doesn't mean I don't understand what needs to be done."

"If you want to live to fulfill your duties, you need to get away," Xander ordered, as he moved toward an old five-gallon bucket, which was the only semi-viable cover. Hector gave him a confused look. Xander looked skyward, but saw that it was already too late because Clade was already tucking his wings to dive. "MOVE!"

Hector finally understood the danger, but it was too little, too late. Clade's jaws grabbed Hector by the scruff before he 'd completed his second step. Without pausing to think, Xander launched himself on top of Clade, sank his rear claws into his disgusting backbone as he hit Clade's head and jammed his front claws into his eyes.

They were already a good six feet above ground when Clade dropped Hector and tried to turn his neck far enough to bite Xander. "YOU!" Clade screeched. "You killed everyone."

"The fire did."

Clade snorted out a big glob of yellow slime, from which Xander ducked.

Wings beating and jaws snapping, Clade flew over the debris-dotted lake, Xander anchored to his back, attention focused on hanging onto the wildly rolling Vi-Purr without impaling himself on the spines projecting from its backbone. He had to figure out a way to control him – the sooner, the better.

But the farther they got away from land, the more he suspected that Clade already had a plan, so Xander flicked his collar to record mode.

Near the center of the lake, Clade began to spiral higher and higher, all the time snarling about how Xander was responsible for killing everyone, freeing the disease that had killed Lucy and Allele, and it was no wonder that Chester hated full-blooded cats so much. With that statement, Clade dove toward a small dark dot in the middle of the lake.

Xander had never felt such speed, nor experienced such clarity of thought, as they shot downward.

He realized Clade was willing to kill himself, if he could take him out at the same time. Clade no longer had anyone to share his life with, so believed his life was no longer worth living.

As the dot gained size and definition, Xander realized Clade was diving toward what appeared to be a dock, which the storm must have torn from its moorings.

Xander reviewed his limited options and a moment before Clade dove headfirst into the sunbaked metal, leaped free. Fighting the instinct to get into position to land feet first, he spread out, as he had once seen a flying squirrel do. Though he still continued to fall, he didn't move quite as fast. Clade crashed into the metal, ricocheted and slammed into the metal, again. Meanwhile, Xander belly-flopped, hard, into the water, driving all the air out of his lungs.

It felt like he kept going down for hours, but after what felt like forever, he admonished himself, I am the Sea Purrtector, the sea is my domain. I will not let water win. He realized he wasn't going anywhere, so began swimming toward the tiny point of light, but no matter how hard he swam, the light didn't seem to get any closer.

His lungs burned for air.

I am the Sea Purrtector, the sea is my domain. I will not let water win.

His body hurt from nose to the tip of this tail.

And still the surface of the lake seemed a lifetime away.

I am the Sea Purrtector, the sea is my domain. I will not let water win.

It was his responsibility to purrtect others and that meant he needed to do something about Allele and Clade's bodies, which meant that he needed to get to that air.

When his nose finally broke the surface, he gasped in air so quickly that he also got a mouth full of water.

Spitting and hissing, he coughed it out then gasped air into his starving lungs.

Slow as the rising sun, his heart rate calmed and he began to breathe normally, then he swam over to the drifting dock and climbed aboard.

As he'd expected, Clade was dead. The force of him hitting the dock had bent the corrugated metal that someone had used to make the top. Why anyone would use that for the deck of a dock was a mystery, but as he looked closer, he realized this wasn't a dock, it was a rectangular piece of roofing off a building.

Xander sat down to study the situation.

He needed to figure out a way to dispose of both potentially contagious Vi-Purrs, but right now, he needed to figure out where Allele was, not to mention calculate how to maneuver this clumsy raft to wherever he needed to go. Worse, the sun was getting higher and he could hear a rooster's morning call rippling over the lake.

As he studied the situation, he spotted something odd sticking out of the water. Squinting, he recognized an upside down bench with a broken leg, which could have possibilities, since it appeared to be made of wood and long enough for Clade's body.

A gust of morning breeze chilled his soggy fur as he leaped back into the cold water and swam to the bench. It was difficult to push it next to the piece of roof, but when he finally got it into position and tried to roll the VI-Purr onto the bench, it tipped over and Clade disappeared into the darkened depths.

Knowing that Hathor had spoken, Xander tipped the bench back, hopped aboard and began to paddle toward the thin column of smoke visible on the distant shore. After a few minutes, he spotted a black trash bag. Altering course, he fished it out, then using the unbroken bench leg, positioned it to catch a tacking breeze toward shore. Slowly, but surely, the bench picked up speed.

Still, it seemed like it was taking forever to sail back.

As he tacked closer, more details became apparent. The smoke was now more of a column than a wisp, and as he stared, there was a whoosh and a ball of fire. That startled him so much that he nearly lost his grip on the garbage bag.

With the fire as a background, he could see that Hector and Scar were moving back and forth on top of the rock where he'd last seen Allele, but the Vi-Purr wasn't there. He frowned as he readjusted his grip on the bag. Were they rolling rocks into the water? No matter how many times he blinked, he couldn't figure out any explanation for their activity.

As the wind began filling the bag, again, he realized that they must have pushed the body off the rock and were now piling small rocks on top of it. It was a brilliant solution, and he hoped that they hadn't had enough contact to catch the flu.

There was a shout on shore, then Mischief and Sharkey were calling his name. He adjusted the bag, so he could better see. With a yowl of delight, Mischief dove into the water and began swimming toward him. Xander steered toward her and soon, she scrambled onto the bench. With a cry of delight, she head-butted him, knocked him over and with mixed purrs and tears, she hugged him, as the bag fluttered away. "I thought you were dead."

"Obviously, you are mistaken."

"You really do know how to swim and surf and stuff."

"Of course I do, I just don't do so, unless it's necessary." He gently maneuvered her off his stomach. "Want to race back to shore?" He rolled into the water and headed for shore, beating her by a good margin.

"Grown men can learn from very little children for the hearts of the little children are pure. Therefore, the Great Spirit may show to them many things which older people miss. Black Elk was smart, wasn't he?" Sharkey's pretty little black and white face was smiling as she rubbed cheeks with him and he was so happy to get back on dry land that he didn't even mind her baffling quotations or Mars whispurring into his ear.

Hector's greeting was more exuberant than he'd expected, but Scar's was the oddest, since he looked like he'd seen the dead rise – purrhaps he'd never seen a cat whose wet fur had dried without proper attention, then had gotten wet, again.

His collar indicated that he had a message.

Knowing he could listen to both his message and the others talking over each other at the same time, he keyed it to play.

"Hey Pal!" Merlin said.

"You nearly gave me heart failure with that dive! Did you plan that or were you just playing it by ear? I mean, I'm glad that Vi-Purr situation is resolved, but your original report should have had photos and a recording of those dreadful things! I can't believe that doctor made them on purpose."

Xander imagined his best friend's emerald green eyes wide with amazement.

"Your sailing technique could use some polish, but since you were dealing with whatever storm debris you could find in the middle of nowhere, even I couldn't have done better.

"By the way, do you realize your collar is still recording to the cloud and I now have proof how the girls feel about you?"

Xander quickly turned off his recording feature.

"Did you ever figure out how much Lucy Fur was involved in Chester's plot? Hector seems like a good guy, and Cheyenne says the Counsel feels better about dealing with him, even though he is a member of the media. They also suggest that you send Sharkey with him for a couple weeks, since she has had Purrtector training and can clue him in when he gets to Santo Domingo – she can help him learn what he needs to do, yadayadayada, then hop a boat to her posting in Puerto Rico, once she's certain he's ready to tackle it on his own.

Merlin lowered his voice, "Hey, Pal, between you and me, Cheyenne gave me the impression that The Counsel wouldn't mind if she stayed in the D R for an extended time – I got the impression that the San Juan posting wasn't as important to them as getting the Dominican Republic's problems sorted out and strange as she can talk, her test scores were top-notch, so you could maybe let her know she's got options.

"Thank Hathor you and the rat took care of that catnip! I still can't believe anyone would be evil enough to target kittens! Good riddance to that Moreau bunch. Later, Pal. Merlin"

Xander's eyes gleamed with amusement over his best friend's phrasing and the way Cheyenne was using Merlin's infatuation with her to give him messages outside Catamondo's normal channels.

Xander swished his tail as he replayed the short message and he smiled.

THE END

I hope you enjoyed The Vi-Purrs. If so, please leave a review on the book's product page. Reviews are very important to authors, so they are greatly appreciated.

Thank you!

Other Books by Jeanne Foguth

Fantasy / Xander's Sea Purrtection Files:

Latitudes & Cattitudes
~ A prequel to the Sea Purrtector Files ~

This short prequel to the Sea Purrtector Files centers on Xander de Hunter when he is a rising star on Catamondo's kick-boxing circuit, with dreams of becoming a Purrtector.

After a match in Seattle, he's asked to help find Cha-Cha, a white Norwegian beauty, who is missing.

With Merlin's assistance, they follow Cha-Cha's trail into the Puget Sound where Xander must face his biggest fear – water.

The Red Claw

Dame Esmeralda, the Purrsident's littermate, has been catnapped. Xander de Hunter, Catamondo's Sea Purrtector hurries to Jamaica to help rescue her, even though Jamaica is one of Dogdom's strongholds. Could this be a trap?

Purr-a-noia

Catamondo and Dogdom's peace treaty is in jeopardy. In Haiti, witchcraft and voodoo seem to be involved in a plot to hex the Purrsident.

Will Xander be able to restore the peace?

The Vi-Purrs

The Daily Mews reports continued violence in the Dominican Republic Purrtectorate.

Xander discovers that the Moreau situation is still affecting the ability of Catamondo to purrtect cats. Worse, the office of the Dominican Republic's Purrtector seems to be involved.

Will Xander be able to restore peace?

Me-YEOW! - coming soon

A possible epidemic is spreading near Mumbai, India and the symptoms are very similar to what Chester Moreau had tried to do in the Dominican Republic. Xander and Mischief fly to India, to make sure no treads of Chester's evil plans still threaten Catamondo.
Will they succeed or will Chester win in the end?

Sci-Fantasy / Kazza's Chatterre Trilogy

Star Bridge

Nimri, an herbal healer and Chatterer's new Keeper of the Peace, must safeguard her tribe from their bitter rivals. To do this, she must find her 'magic core'.
Many light years away, Colonel Larwin Atano, an elite Guerreterre Shadow Warrior, fights to save his intergalactic star-fighter. Despite all efforts, he crashes.
Larwin perceives Chatterre's resources as a means to gain power and prestige and views the planet's inhabitants as a minor inconvenience.
Nimri believes Larwin is a supernatural Guardian, who will protect her tribe from their rivals.
Who will survive the coming conflict?

Thunder Moon

Thunder Cartwright dreams that madrox (dragons) will invade Chatterre and destroy his world unless the star bridge is closed.
Raine, a Kalamaran Dragon Shepard, must catch a rogue mooncalf

and return it to the herd or face possible death.
Who will win and who will die?

Fire Island

Tem-aki Atano fell through a rift when the star bridge was destroyed, and must find a way to survive on an island, which worships destructive madrox (dragons).
Cameron O'Ryan must figure out if legend and reality have things in common or merely are stories told to children.
Meanwhile three dragon eggs are hatching... Will they destroy the island and everyone living on it? Or can they be controlled?

Contemporary Suspense/Romance

Deadly Rumors

Kelsey MacLennan and Devlin Doran both want to make the world better.
Doran believes the rumors about the MacLennans dealing drugs, so his goal is to bring them down.
Kelsey MacLennan wants to make the world better, but her senatorial political campaign turns deadly and rumors abound, when the incumbent must win or be killed by his backers. Devlin Doran's younger sister died of an overdose, so his goal is to prosecute pushers. Rumors abound that the MacLennans are high in the local drug network and he is targeting Kelsey MacLennan.
Will they be able to separate fact from fiction or will the rumors be deadly?

Fatal Attractions

Ariel and Tempest Danner have escaped Tempest's homicidal father for the sixth time in five years. Armed with new identities and disguises, they are determined that Fairbanks, Alaska will be a sanctuary where they can live in peace.

Stone O'Banyon, their new landlord, has been divorced for three years. All his energy is focused on his job and Dolly, who would never hurt him.

The last thing Ariel needs or wants is the attraction she feels for another tall, dark man, who seems hard as the granite he is named for, but the fascination will not go away. Stone isn't any happier with his obsessive thoughts concerning Ariel.

Things seem calm, then Ariel and Tempest catch sight of the man they had hoped they would never encounter and things turn fatal...again.

Passion's Fire

Prior to the blaze that killed her husband, Jacqueline Cardew believed he wrote the 'fiery messages' she received. Now she finds a new note inside her locked house. Jacqueline suspects her faceless stalker murdered Adam and she is next. She flees north, where she joins Link Gavallan's group on a two week long Alaskan wilderness canoe trip. As they float down the desolate river, she receives another message...

Instead of finding a sanctuary, has she made it easier for her stalker to trap her?

Connect with Jeanne Foguth

Though Jeanne began her career technical writing, her love of romantic-suspense, whether it be present, future or in an unknown galaxy, inspired her to write the novels she wanted to find in bookstores. Since marrying, Jeanne and her husband have lived from the arctic to the tropics, as well as from yacht to off-grid mountain home. She loves using vivid colors and flowing shapes in her oil paintings as well as creating edible landscapes. She recently finished preparing previously-published novels for their digital debut, and is now working on new stories.

You can always find out what she is working on and/or contact her at:

Her blog: http://foguth.wordpress.com

Her web-home: http://www.jeannefoguth.com/

Facebook: https://www.facebook.com/jeannefoguth

OR follow on Twitter @JeanneFoguth

www.ingramcontent.com/pod-product-compliance
Lightning Source LLC
Chambersburg PA
CBHW071310130626
46556CB00004B/1543